To Dear
Rosa

Jon Christenson

Flights of Fancy

Flights of Fancy

❖

Jon Christensen

To order additional copies of this book, contact:
Xlibris Corporation
1-888-795-4274
www.Xlibris.com
Orders@Xlibris.com
27774

Contents

Foreword ix

The Maddok Destiny 1

The Bath Tub 54

2026-2040
    A New Beginning 60

Dick and Jane 75

The Key to Contentment 81

Ponderings in Paranoia and other food for thought 88

Dedication

This book is dedicated
to
my wife, Lyn,
whose constructive criticism
provided encouragement,
and with thanks to
my long time friend, Bruce Fyvie,
whose thoughts provided some inspiration
for The Maddok Destiny.

FOREWORD

This little book of short stories (with one novelette) has a genre range that goes from horror fiction to speculative fiction to something I'm not sure there's a name for (as in Ponderings in Paranoia). I'm afraid the readers will be left to define the genre for themselves. I'm sure that the definition will depend on whether the reader takes the subject matter as tongue-in-cheek or finds a modicum of wisdom in it. Anyway, and in that regard, it is in part a project book in which readers, should they feel motivated, may be left with a task to perform.

As to the inspiration for some of these stories, I certainly have to give credit to writers like Stephen King and Dean Koontz; although they likely wouldn't thank me for *blaming* them for this. Also, that late, great horror genre writer, Edgar Allan Poe, had a great influence on me. My hope is that his influence will show up in its best light in the introductory lyrical ditties of 'The Maddok Destiny'.

With regard to 'The Maddok Destiny', I've tried to imbue it with something of the flavour of 19th century prose. I've tempered that flavour a little in hopes that it shouldn't seem too stiff while maintaining something of that *sepia* sense. Because the story covers several centuries, as it goes forward in time the reader may notice that the style of prose alters subtly to a more 20th century feel. I think that the effort was successful and I hope the reader can agree.

'The Maddok Destiny' is a story, of novelette length, that touches on the occult and demonology; but basically it's a story about the struggle and eventual conquest of good over evil within one family.

'The Bath Tub' is a short horror story about a couple who eventually acquire a house that they can fashion into a home. The wife buys a very unusual, antique bath tub. They eventually discover exactly how unusual it really is.

'2026-2040—A New Beginning' is a short story, set in the near future, about a boy whose extraordinary, innate intelligence drives him to create a better life for himself than what he sees around him. Born into a time of global economic chaos, he feels that his goal can only be achieved by using his intellect as ruthlessly as it will allow. He finally discovers that, intellect notwithstanding, he is only human after all.

'Dick and Jane' is a short murder-with-a-touch-of-horror story about a young couple who are love's young dream personified. Then, after the birth of their daughter, things start falling apart for them. Disaster strikes from within. But if it hadn't come from within, it may well have come from without.

'The Key to Contentment' is an account, by a self-proclaimed genius, of how he would bring total contentment to Mankind—if only *they* would listen.

'Ponderings in Paranoia—and other food for thought' is a collection of some ideas that could be cause for paranoia, or merely food for thought. This collection ends with some real food for thought in the form of an ancient riddle that I came across while travelling in England. No one seemed to know who first penned it; and in my extensive search, I never found out either.

Finally, it's my hope that there may be something in this book for most people to enjoy; and that my decision to assemble a mixed genre collection wasn't total lunacy after all. So please read on and come to your own determination, whatever that may be.

Jon Christensen.

THE MADDOK DESTINY

PART I

GENESIS

The Prologue

The birth of evil
Begins with pain,
That its demon sire
May live again.

Begin thy reign
Imbued in blood
And continue on
In a cursed flood.

It was said that the roots of the Maddok family tree had germinated from out the loins of Morgwyn; Morgwyn the Mad dog of Malevale. It was, if true, a most unholy germination indeed. Morgwyn, whose debaucheries were legendary, was indeed a mad dog—and worse—much worse.

It was known that he had sired no fewer than twenty children; seven of whom were with his own daughters and two with a grand daughter. But that was merely incest, and incest was the least reprehensible of his deeds.

Morgwyn, at something approaching six and a half feet tall was, for the times, a giant of a man with a physical strength and temper to match. His square not unbecoming face was framed with a curly tousle of beard and hair the colour of ancient pewter, and his glacier grey eyes were said to hold a charm that at once could seem to mezmerize and to terrify.

Morgwyn's one and only *legal* wife, Gwythlyn, was as good as he was evil. But alas, in those days, a woman had as much to say about whom she married as she had about the phases of the moon. Gwythlyn the Good was a gentle creature with a good mind and a quick wit. A petite and lovely figure of a woman, her inner strength was not at first apparent; but extant it must have been for her to have endured the years of life that she did with Morgwyn.

Their complete contradistinctions in nature and physical stature notwithstanding, Morgwyn treated Gwythlyn with a consideration that could have passed for civility, given evidence of his dealings with others of either gender or any age. He did enjoy his coitus extentum, though, and hardly a night would pass that, upon preparing to retire, Gwythlyn would not hear the all too familiar:

"Wife, by the horns of Astaroth, take thee unto thyself the horn of Morgwyn. Come, come! Hye thyself! The night doth wane."—And after a few hours, he would be sated enough to sleep through what remained of the night.

Finally, though, his outrages aroused such overwhelming disgust (Morgwyn was not particularly discreet) that the villagers were forced to overcome their considerable fear of his formidable wrath and banish him from their midst. To accommodate procurement of another home, not only did he have to travel some considerable distance, but change his name as well.

The latter necessity came at a fortuitous epoch for Morgwyn. At about that time, registration of citizenry required the official acquisition and use of surnames. It was a simple enough matter to transmute Mad Dog to Maddok, which was accomplished with alacrity. Morgwyn was satisfied; the bureaucrats, never ones for involved procedures, were satisfied; and all was well with his new situation.

However, the peace could no more endure for long than could Morgwyn change his character. Before long, he again ran afoul of the local citizenry. This time, however, it was far more serious. Not only had community morals been flouted and outraged, but a life had been lost during one of Morgwyn's more bestial debauches. During the course of unnatural coitus with a boy barely seventeen, Morgwyn had strangled him to death in an effort to stifle his screams.

Morgwyn had subsequently fallen into a drunken slumber and was discovered in flagrant delecto some time hence by the boy's father. The father may well have met with foul play himself had not his cries for help been answered by a deputation of village men. Arriving just in time to arrest such an eventuality, they managed, through prodigious effort, to incarcerate Morgwyn until such time as a magistrate could attend.

Morgwyn Maddok's trial was an open air affair to accommodate the crowd that had gathered for it. The prisoner, shackled hand a foot, stood on a high, raised platform flanked by two of the sturdiest gaolers that the district was able to procure. The platform was ringed with pikemen pointing long, steel tipped pikes in the general direction of the prisoner.

From his vantage point, Morgwyn glowered down upon the strangely silent crowd and the magistrate. Some individuals in the crowd were only occasionally successful in dodging the gobs of gelatinous spittle that flew from his frothing mouth. None, however, were successful in dodging the verbal vitriol that accompanied the spittle.

"Thou hast been found guilty of bestial and unnatural acts; heinous crimes against the sensibilities of civilized society, not the least of which be the wilful murder of a human; and consorting with demonic forces and entities, which hath all and duly been witnessed by certain of the good citizens of this community. Therefore wilt thou hence be taken and gaoled until market day next, and thence shalt thou be conducted to the market square, where, at twelve of the clock, shalt thou be hung, drawn and quartered as prescribed by the law," said the magistrate in what, incredibly, seemed to be one breath.

"Ye'll all be roasting in Hades afore the butcher's crescent tastes of my guts," shrieked Morgwyn.

With that, he hurtled headlong from the raised platform, taking his two gaolers with him. The three were immediately impaled by the phalanx of guards' pikes upon which they fell. The gaolers succumbed almost instantly, but Morgwyn clung tenaciously to life, cursing and reviling his captors without respite. Then, in the early morning of market day, he too expired with these few words:

"I told ye, ye pious progeny of shyte! Receive me now, O lord of darkness!"

With the death of Morgwyn, Gwythlyn the Good took herself off to a convent and spent the rest of her years in contemplation of her shame and degradation in utter silence.

Three of her four living sons were eventually hung for sorcery. The fourth, Morgyn, became a monk and something of a healer. He spent the rest of his life bringing succour to lepers.

The three daughters with whom Morgwyn had sired a total of seven children, eventually succumbed to what today would have been diagnosed as syphilis; not, however, before producing several more offspring amongst them. The fourth, Teulyna, accompanied her mother to the convent where she eventually became prioress.

The granddaughter, Agwelyn, with whom Morgwyn had sired two children, went on to the dubious distinction of becoming a renowned courtesan, referred to in hushed whispers as the whore of Wencisbradt. This distinction, however, was to be cut short in her twenty-fourth year when she too was hung for sorcery as well as the murders of three barons and a duke.

It is told how the adage: 'never does the apple fall far from the tree' was first coined by the magistrate who pronounced sentence of death upon Agwelyn Maddok.

There were certainly no grey areas in the lives or deeds of the early Maddok family members; black or white, pit or pinnacle.

Thus was the genesis of the Maddok dynasty. Some Maddoks were kind and gentle (no doubt a genetic reflection of Gwythlyn's nature), but a goodly percentage were, while not as evil and profligate as Morgwyn, certainly inclined to the dissolute side of human nature. The final destiny of the family, still some centuries in the future, was to reflect this duality in a most remarkable way.

The Dark Ages were indeed dark, not only in thought and deed, but in culture and all its components. This dark period coursed not only through societies in general, but through the Maddok dynasty in particular. Into this dark age flooded the unrecorded progeny of the Maddoks, bringing with it all the cultist evil that mankind had stored and nurtured in its tortured psyche since the beginning of time.

These generations of the Maddoks are genealogically known as the 'lost generations'. Nothing concrete is known of individual Maddoks throughout this period. However, given their genesis, one thing may reasonably be ascertained: if anything of exceptionally evil import occurred, it could be earmarked as Maddok in origin.

Such names as Vladimir 'The Impaler', the Borgias, De Sade, Grigori Yefimovich (more commonly known as Rasputin) and many more of that ilk are said to have descended from Maddok blood lines. At the same time, however, it should be noted that Nostradamus was said to have been a direct descendant of Morgyn Maddok, who, before he took the monastic oath, had fathered a son with a wife who died in childbirth.

It can be seen, therefore, that although evil was a dominant factor in Maddok genetics, it was by no means predominant. The good that filtered down from Gwythlyn's genes remained intact to the end of the Maddok line. The evil eventually just destroyed itself.

It has been said that the lust for power is as strong as the lust for sexual gratification; and that *power* itself is the strongest of aphrodesiacs. It can be little wonder, then, that the driving force behind the evil permeating the Maddok dynasty maintained such a long and rapacious life, and that the rampant depravity became so ingrained. What is a wonder, though, is that the spark of goodness wasn't completely extinguished early on. That the goodness survived long enough to be passed on to a succeeding line of the family bears testimony to the innate goodness of the human spirit.

However, I do but o'er-leap myself. You must peruse what follows to better be able to judge for yourself.

> Then darkness came hard
> Upon all the land;
> A darkness known best
> By the Maddok clan.
>
> Their spawn did spread,
> Of the blackest kind;
> A blackness known only
> By the bestial mind.
>
> Into that vale
> That evil doth know,
> The lost generations
> Must surely go.

PART II

MADDOK

Think only on the lessons
Your past has taught;
Dwell not on the sorrows
It may have wrought.

There is no tomorrow
To those who sorrow
For yesterday.

CHAPTER I

The snow fell in hushed whispers, draping itself like a glistening ivory mantle about the shingled shoulders of the still little house.

Inside, a coffee purcolator burbled cheerily, adding richly to the overall delicious aroma of the cozy kitchen. The oversized and time blackened woodburning stove hosted an odd assortment of bubbling, sizzling and lid bobbing pots and pans on its ample cast iron surface.

In the spacious livingroom, a fire blazed and crackled warmly in a large fieldstone fireplace. The fire cast flickering shadows over an amber bearskin rug stretched before it in a sea of well groomed fur. The opposite wall was fairly festooned with animal trophies. Hides, horns and heads hung in symmetrical spleandour, seemingly still alive in the flickering light emanating from the rustic hearth.

The peace of this tranquil setting was occasionally nudged by a soft snore rising from the bearded face of a recumbent figure, dozing on a leather chaise in the warm glow of the hearth fire. After a time, the tranquility was more rudely nudged by the insistent voice of old Ben, an ancient, oak cased grandfather clock that chose then, in time honoured tradition, to announce the hour in deliberate and precisely spaced tones from its hammer-struck brass gong. It methodically struck eight times and then fell silent and took its rest. Took its rest save for the clack of its internal mechanism, the ponderous swing of its large, gleaming pendulum and the almost imperceptible movement of the burnished brass hands across its lacquered ivory face.

At the first of old Ben's strokes, the dozing figure was fairly catapulted into complete consciousness. Eyeing the old time piece fondly, James Arthur Maddok (Maddy to his friends) fluidly swung his long, sinewous frame to a standing position and stretched languorously until his finger tips were brushing the low ceiling timbers. He then leisurely sauntered through to the kitchen, arriving just in time to rescue his sizzling supper from incineration.

After savouring his repast to the last delicious morsel, he tilted back his chair and emitted a hearty belch in appreciation of yet another culinary delight, prepared by he knew not whom.

Then they struck! From seemingly everywhere and with galvanic energy, grim and grotesque gorgons of a bygone era leapt upon him; shrieking, tearing, tattering and devouring until nothing remained save blood soaked shreds of what had once, very recently, been clothing.

The feast, it was agreed, was always so much more fulfilling when the meal had, itself, just dined and was completely relaxed and satisfied . . .

Maddy awoke with a start as old Ben struck the first of nine strokes. Although it was very warm and he was bathed in perspiration, he found himself trembling uncontrollably. It had been the same hideous dream that he had experienced—how many times? The same hideous and all too life-like dream.

It had all started, he recalled, shortly after he had inherited this quaint little bungalow from his great uncle, Andrew Angus Maddok, some two months previously. Until then, he had quite contentedly eked out a comfortable living as a stock agent for a curio shop in the city. He'd had only faint memories of stories he'd heard as a child concerning sometimes mad, sometimes weird but always eccentric old uncle Andrew.

Andrew Maddok had, it seems, dabbled in some form of sorcery, so the stories went, and had run afoul of some power or other shortly before his demise. Some weeks before his sudden death, his demeanor and visage had taken on a distinctly troubled and haunted aspect; and although he had been something of a recluse, rumours and speculations as to the possible causes of this change ran rampant through the nearby village.

What had alerted the villagers that something may be seriously amiss at the Maddok bungalow, was the report by a passing itinerant of shrieks of a most hideous nature emanating from that abode. A premonition of disaster had immediately gripped the villagers, and within twenty minutes a dozen or more of them had ascended to the site only to find complete and eerie silence, and any access securely barred.

The singularly strange thing about Andrew's ending was the apparent vicious brutality involved, which clearly indicated foul play of the most heinous kind. This, coupled with the fact that Andrew had barricaded himself inside the house to the extent that it took six men with the aid of a length of sturdy birch to batter down the door, made for a monumental mystery. Egress and ingress had so completely been precluded that had Andrew not been savaged to death, he could quite foreseeably have suffocated.

Due to the obvious bestial savagery inflicted, there had been very little remaining of the body to actually identify as being that of Andrew Maddok. Save for a few shreds of barely identifiable clothing, a few bone fragments and a heavy copper bracelet with six pentagonal lode stones fastened around its surface, nothing of Andrew remained. The latter article had positively been identified, by several, as having belonged to Andrew Maddok.

Another curious conundrum was that, despite the very obvious violence, the rest of the interior and furnishings remained unmoved and unmolested.

Over the fetid aura of death was the unmistakeable odour of overcooked and distinctly burnt food. Upon inspection, it had been discovered that the kitchen table had been set for a solitary diner. Upon the stove, oddly enough quite cold and devoid even of embers, sat an assortment of pots and pans. While those pots and pans had once contained food in the process of being cooked, they then contained only the charred remnants of what must once have been a quite palatable and definitely substantial repast. Some, then present, took a cursory note of all this, thought it more than a bit peculiar and then quite simply dismissed it, because, after all, Andrew had been mad—hadn't he?

An autopsy had been foregone for lack of anything substantial enough to perform one on. A brief inquest was adjourned after it had been tacitly agreed that *things like these* were best left unprobed, and a verdict of *death by misadventure* was entered into the district records.

Although the reasons were never questioned or even discussed, it had been generally decided that to inter whatever remained of Andrew Maddok in a leaden acid pottle might be a more than prudent design.

All this having been accomplished, everyone settled down to speculate as to what would, should or could be done by way of the disposition of the Maddok property.

CHAPTER II

Time trod tirelessly on and the glow of the Maddok *incident* furtively faded from the public memory. Then one day, Maddy arrived to claim his inheritance. Rumour and supposition were reawakened. New colour and twists were woven into the Maddok incident. Would the grand nephew liquidate the property and move on (secretly, it was hoped not); would he settle in—and take up where the old man had left off (no one really knew what that might be)—and to what chilling outcome would it lead? The populace was fairly atingle with secret curiosity and anticipation.

The villagers were to be disappointed and disillusioned, however. In contrast to his eccentric great uncle, James Maddok was a quiet, unprepossessing individual. He had an air about him that invited friendliness, though. Perhaps it was his quick, easy smile that displayed such white, even teeth; or perhaps his warm politeness, not displayed merely out of shyness but from a sincere appreciation of recognition. There was also something almost sad about Maddy that invited something akin to a protective attitude. Despite their secret disappointment, the villagers could not help but accept this tall, rather lanky stranger as one of their community.

The only similarities to the late Maddok were some familial likeness about the eyes, the artistic cut of the beard and a distinction of gait that resembled nothing so much as a blend of limp and seaman's swagger.

At first, Maddy happily busied himself with provisioning his new home, cutting firewood for the oncoming winter, effecting a few minor repairs to the house, cleaning and just generally setting up house. However, as weeks passed, Maddy began to find the stillness of the little house increasingly tiresome; almost oppressive. Coupled with disquieting dreams and inexplicable occurrances within the house, the solitude that he had at first sought out finally became too much to bear.

He decided that perhaps he should advertise in the village for someone—not a constant companion, but a housekeeper. Someone just to come in periodically to clean the house and to break the stillness of the place. Maddy, after all, was something more by way of being sociable than, by any stretch, his late uncle had ever been; and occasional company would be agreeable.

It happened that during conversation with some villagers, the widow Emiline Herrik's name and circumstances were mentioned. She had, it was said, been having some small difficulty feeding and housing herself and her five children. Her husband, it was revealed, had perished some few years earlier in a mining mishap. As she certainly had her hands full taking in laundry and sewing, it was suggested that perhaps she wouldn't be opposed to her eldest daughter, fifteen year old Kristine, earning a bit of her own keep.

Keeping sensitively to the proper protocol in such matters, Maddy prevailed upon the village clergyman to approach the widow Emiline and broach the proposal of hiring her daughter for a few days a week (for perhaps an overgenerous salary). Emiline was ecstatic and without reservation at the prospect of another income for the household. She insisted, though, that for the named salary the girl should work for at least a few hours every day. This being agreeable to Maddy, Kristine was sent to begin work on the following day.

Kristine Herrik was quietly coquettish and abundantly aware of her prematurely burgeoning womanhood. A fine lithe figure, long ebon hair, large green crystalline eyes and full red lips under an impurtinently turned up nose all blended into a package of seemingly innocent sensuality. She was perhaps overanxious to test all of her developing charms on any not unbecoming male at hand; and now it seemed that James Maddok was more becoming and more at hand than most.

Kristine bode her time for a few days, and displayed, in the meantime and at every opportunity, her obvious femininity for Maddy's benefit. After a time, it appeared to her that her sometimes not too subtle wiles were having the desired effect upon their target. If only he had not been so maddeningly preoccupied with the maintenance of, and general tinkering with that enormous old time piece, it might not have taken so long, she thought.

Old Ben, Maddy had told her, had come to be like a friend to him. It was of the utmost importance, he had said with an odd look, that Ben always be preened to perfection. She had shrugged this off as merely an eccentricity; but his words and that look on his face kept resurfacing from the back of her mind to intrigue her further. The clock had been the only household furnishing that he had brought with him from the city; and it did appear that there was something akin to friendship in Maddy's relationship to it. It seemed, to the girl, a strange fixation indeed.

Maddy, while completely unaware of Kristine's overt manipulations to attract him, was nevertheless drawn to her as he had never been drawn to another in all of his thirty-six years. He was keenly aware of the disparity in their ages and that he was in a position of some trust, but the uncontrollable attraction was there notwithstanding.

He managed, though, to control himself physically and was at some pains to make certain that none but the most casual and necessary physical contacts occurred. Even those innocent contacts, however, seemed to have an unusually heady effect upon him. He assured himself that as long as no contact more lingering chanced to happen then his unaccountable attraction could be kept in check; and things continued in this vein for some time.

Kristine had taken to preparing a table for Maddy's midday meal before leaving for home. Although this was not really any part of her duties, she did not mind in the least. It gave her a little more time to practise her wiles and to angle for a more meaningful physical contact. She knew that he had been deliberately and very maddeningly careful about these contacts. By this time Kristine had succumbed to her own little trap and now wanted him desperately.

She was standing on a stool in order to reach the cupboard shelf upon which the dishes were kept when she saw a chance to culminate this frustrating little game. Maddy had just entered the kitchen and was about to pass behind her on his way to the wash stand. Kristine feigned a stumble, tipped the stool in the process and tumbled towards him. Maddy instictively extended his arms and she, with a half turn of olympic perfection, adroitly attained her goal.

In that instant, as he held her securely in his arms, she unexpectedly grasped his head between her two hands and kissed him full on the mouth. The kiss, ardent, passionate and demanding, stirred something very primal within Maddy.

Something else now held sway over Maddy's actions. He carried her purposefully through to the livingroom and there they slowly sank into the welcoming depths of the bearskin rug, still locked lasciviously together.

There, on that rug, bathed in the flickering glow of the hearth fire and under the vacant stares of the heads upon the wall, seemingly hours were spent in feverish exploration and excitation of each other's animalistically aroused bodies. When, finally, they were both physically and emotionally drained and spent, they fell into a sound slumber still entwined in each other's embrace.

Old Ben dutifully sounded three times and Maddy awoke with a start. He stared incredulously first at Kristine's nakedness, then at his own, then at the roughly strewn clothing about them. He was thunderstruck by what he knew had obviously transpired, though he had only a very faint recollection of any of it.

As he gently disengaged himself from Kristine's embrace to begin reclothing himself, she slowly awoke and stretched languorously. She smiled broadly to herself as she observed Maddy's reparations through still half shut eyelids.

When Maddy became aware that Kristine was no longer asleep, he stammered out profuse apologies and self incriminations for what had occurred. He solemnly vowed to her that if she would only forgive him such a thing would never ever happen again; to which she replied that if that was the case, she would never forgive him. With that, she threw on her scattered clothing, gave the bewildered Maddy a quick kiss on the cheek and skipped out of the door and towards home, humming a bright little ditty all the way.

Maddy did not know quite what to make of the girl's response, but he vowed to himself, as he buffed old Ben's case, what he had already vowed to Kristine. It must definitely never happen again. What a shameful disaster it would be, especially for poor, gentle Kristine, if anyone should ever find out about their impulsive indiscretion. Her reputation would be blighted for life; although she did not seem overly concerned herself. But she was, after all, little more than a child, albeit in a very womanly body. Maddy shook his head to try and dispel the all too vivid image of that sweet, young—oh so young and oh so sweet—body. Maddy buffed all the more vigorously.

CHAPTER III

Emiline Herrik noticed distinct changes in her eldest daughter's demeanour. No longer was Kristine sullen and disagreeable. She was now of radiant spirit and even helpful about the house. Her countenance verily glowed, and she hummed or sang almost constantly in accompaniment to whatever she was doing.

Emiline harboured some suspicions that this drastic change in temperament might be at least partly due to a younger girl's infatuation with an older man. James Maddok, she thought, was perhaps somewhat old for her daughter, though a pleasant enough fellow both in nature and in looks. She could well understand such an infatuation, if such was the case.

Maybe it had nothing to do with infatuation, she thought, as she tried to dispel the notion. Maybe it was only the new responsibility and sudden sense of worth that had brought about such welcome and dramatic changes.

Whatever the reason, the ends seemed to justify the means to Emiline. They were living comfortably for the first time in ever such a long time. She had even been able to put by a little bit of money for some extras for her children. The poor darlings had done without so many things for so long, she thought.

The widow had wanted to reciprocate for Maddy's kindness and generousity by having him over for an evening meal, and to get to know him better. Time and again, however, he would offer a reason for not venturing out for the evening. These refusals were always accompanied by sincere apologies so that Emiline would not be made to feel as though her or her family's company would not be anything but agreeable.

Maddy himself could not understand the reason for the refusals. Oddly enough, it was not because of the embarrassment and guilt he would have felt in the widow's presence. He would find himself determined to accept the next invitation, only to find that it had come and that he had again refused.

Maddy was not worldly wise or sophisticated in the least concerning matters dealing with the occult; but he did realize that there had to be some connection between his involuntary refusals of the widow's dinner invitations and his own mysteriously prepared evening meals. It was as though someone or something wanted him to be at home in the evenings; for whatever purpose he couldn't even hazard a guess.

He would invariably become drowsy at about half past six in the evening and fall sound asleep shortly thereafter. Old Ben would waken him at eight o'clock, and his meal would be ready and the table set. After the meal was finished, he would doze again until old Ben woke him at nine o'clock. It was during these latter dozing episodes that that hideous dream would usually occur—not always, but usually.

Irrespective of how the rest of his day had progressed, or what he had done with his time, this seemed to have become a preordained timetable for the evening. His only ally in all of this seemed to be the ancient clock that always woke him up just before—before what?

Maddy had read through and pored over all of his late uncle's copious notes, manuscripts, letters and books countless times trying to find some answer, some clue, some thread of intelligence that may explain the apparently inexplicable. But amongst the chaotic clutter of the Maddok library nothing could be found that would have provided an illuminative insight into this mystery.

In the cramped attic library there was also a strange assortment of paraphernalia for the performance of occult rites. Amongst the curious goblets, sinister looking daggers, candelabras in wonderously warped and twisted designs, jar upon jar of evil smelling powders, roots and only heaven (or hell) knew what else, Maddy had discovered his uncle's copper bracelet.

This item alone, for some unconscious reason, he had taken downstairs with him. He polished it to a high lustre and placed it on the mantle closest to old Ben. There it caught the reflected hearth light and gleamed in answer, as though it had a life of its own. The six pentagonal lode stones now stood out in stark contrast to the newly burnished surface.

Eventually Maddy gave up on trying to solve a riddle that was apparently insolvable. Instead he decided to make an earnest effort to break the evening cycle that he had allowed himself to become entrenched in. After all, habits could be broken—couldn't they? He felt he must at least try. His sanity, if not his very life, may depend upon it, he thought; then he shook his head at the seeming melodrama of the very idea.

Meanwhile, another concern had intruded itself upon his already troubled thoughts. Old Ben had begun to behave strangely; erratically. The time piece began to lose an inordinate amount of time; sometimes ten or fifteen minutes a day. Sometimes it would sound as though it was about to stop completely. Always, then, its formerly regular ticking would sound somehow laboured, as though the mechanism was seriously struggling to keep active.

All of Maddy's efforts to correct this irregular behaviour were proving futile. He was finding that the time would have to be corrected two or three times during the course of the day. By the morning, it would have fallen behind by as much as twenty minutes.

A mild panic began to set in. What if it stopped completely? What if it stopped while he slept? What if it stopped while he was dozing after—? Maddy tried to shake off what he felt may be an irrational fear. It was only a dream, after all. He would try and put his mind to other things.

Maddy had once contemplated selling the bungalow and moving to the village. The terms of his late uncle's trust fund had stipulated, however, that the monetary allowance would continue only while the beneficiary occupied the house. This, Maddy thought, had been a strange and, as it turned out, an inconvenient insistence. It was not as though the Maddok house was an ancestral manor, in the usual sense of the term.

In the end, Maddy had satisfied himself that no one would have wanted to buy it in any event; not given its recent grisly history. He would merely have to stay put and endure as long as the trust fund endured. He fervently hoped that it wouldn't be too long. He found himself thinking in fond terms of his life in the city; something he never dreamed that he would ever do. His beloved grandmother's favourite lines came to him at these times:

"There is no tomorrow to those who sorrow for yesterday." Strange, that after so many years, he should recall those words now, he would think.

CHAPTER IV

Spring was now fast upon the district. The trees of the valley orchards were festooned with blossoms that turned their petalled faces to the warming sun. New grass now carpeted the gentle hillsides and the last of the snowdrops now gave way to newly blooming crocuses and budding daffodils. Everything was alive and fresh again. The cold drafts of winter now turned to gentle, fragrant breezes of spring. Everywhere birds sang and small woodland creatures chattered a welcome to the renewed life of nature.

Kristine had been mildly disturbed, upon reflection, at the wild, carnal sensuality of her first real sexual encounter. However, as she recalled the mingled sensations, the pure ecstacy of it all, the disturbing aspects magically melted away. She longingly looked forward to further encounters; and surely, then, Maddy must feel the same way, she thought.

She was sadly disappointed to discover that Maddy did not seem to share her fondest ambition. She would simply have to play the part of huntress again. This tended only to heighten her hedonistic excitement.

Patience and persistent cunning reaped the desired results for her in the days and weeks to follow. On three occassions she succeeded in seducing the hapless, innately gullible, Maddy; who, after each carnal coupling, would again renew his vows and efforts of celibacy concerning this young succubus incarnate. Yet each encounter would be followed by another, and would be more wanton and abandoned to lust than the one before.

Maddy seemed to have little control over his will in these situations, but the guilt and remorse he felt afterwards were genuine and heartfelt. Finally he could tolerate the growing guilt no longer. He decided that the solitude would be so much easier to bear than the thought of the sexual usery continuing. So, in the gentlest manner possible, and not without pangs of remorse, he dismissed Kristine from service.

He tried to assuage her tearful disappointment by telling her some fabrication about requiring complete solitude to set some business affairs in order. Finally, the offer of a month's salary as payment for the sudden termination of employment seemed to settle her sobs somewhat.

Although Maddy could not quite forgive himself for what had passed between them, he did feel relieved that the temptation for any recurrence was now well and truly out of the way; and that, inasmuch as no one in the village had become aware of their indiscretions, Kristine's reputation was still intact.

As time passed, Kristine began noticing certain physical changes taking place. It had started with nausea that would awaken her from a sound slumber. Eventually, these bouts would leave her prostrate until late morning. Then too, although her appetite had diminished, she found herself filling her clothing out rather more than usual. The once lissom figure was now definitely rounding out.

Neither had these changes escaped her mother's notice. Emiline's concern soon mingled with suspicion and she sent for the village physician. The suspicions were soon rendered into fact by the physician's diagnosis. Kristine, it seemed, was four to five months gone with child.

Although Emiline alternately demanded, wheedled and entreated her daughter to divulge who the father might be, Kristine steadfastly remained silent on the subject. It was, after all, a predicament of her own creation, she thought. During the time after her abrupt dismissal from Maddy's service, or perhaps because of it, she had outgrown her infatuation with him; and by now certainly did not wish to be forced into sharing her child with him.

Emiline, out of habit due to her eldest daughter's wilful precocity, had always kept a close watch on her. She knew full well whom Kristine had associated with and when. She had, therefore, come to the conclusion that there was only one man upon whom the guilt for the deed could justifiably be laid to rest. However, without her daughter's cooperation in the matter, Emiline, in all good conscience, could not bring herself to accuse such a well liked figure of their little community of such a gross breach of trust.

The sands of time trickled on. Summer turned to golden autumn and harvest time came and went. Then the first chill winds of winter were once again upon them, and the first silent snows began scudding from swollen, billowing clouds. The fields and bare limbed trees and rolling hills became cloaked in ermine that twinkled on moonbright nights as though a net of countless diamonds had been cast over all.

On one hill overlooking the little village, the Maddok house nestled securely against a backdrop of snow laced birch. All was quiet now save for the anxious pacing of the master of that house. Old Ben's last laboured tick had been heard on the previous day, and seemingly nothing could be done to reanimate the recalcitrant old time piece. Maddy had not slept since that last tick and was enveloped by an unshakeable foreboding that he dared not voice, even to himself.

In the village a piercing, agonized shriek shattered the stillness of the night. A light flickered to life in a window of the Herrik house. Emiline, carrying her lamp, rushed to the room that Kristine shared with her two younger sisters. Wide awake now, Emiline still was little prepared for the sight that greeted her as she opened the door.

In the centre of Kristine's winter quilt was a large scarlet design that had not been there previously. It glistensed with a liquid lustre in the lamplight as the figure on the bed writhed and convulsed. Kristine's scream once again pierced the air as the two terrified sisters cowered on the far side of their own bed.

Emiline summoned her eldest son and told him to go and rouse the physician and to bring him straight away. In the meantime Kristine had to be bound hand and foot to the bedstead to restrain her from tearing at herself. She frothed and writhed and cursed and spat like someone possessed. Her mother was beside herself with anguish for her daughter's agony and distress. She had never seen or heard of anyone suffering so in childbirth—and the blood, what of all that blood?

Finally the physician arrived. Upon seeing what lay before him, he immediately stripped to the waist and bagan to work on his unfortunate patient. He first sedated her with an ancient and potent nostrum, and then began trying to speed up the birthing process so that he might then attempt to staunch the hemorrhaging.

Eventually, at about daybreak, the offspring arrived. The physician and Emiline gasped in unison. The—*child* was groteque. It resembled a human baby only in that it had a small body, a large head and four limbs. The body was covered in horny, greyish skin. There was a multitude of bony protuberances on its bald pate, and the face— especially the eyes—were beyond the power of ordinary description. The digits on hands and feet alike were long and curved and clawlike—and webbed. The infant emitted something resembling a gurgling growl and then expired with a trickle of putrescent liquid oozing and bubbling from its lipless mouth.

The physician's attempts at staunching Kristine's hemorrhage were finally successful; however, it did not in the least diminish Death's success. Kristine peacefully slipped the bonds of life and suffered no more.

Emiline had to be sedated and the physician's wife summoned to see to the children's needs. Later that afternoon, when she was once again coherent, Emiline related her suspicions to the village elders. After some lengthy debate, it was decided that a small delegation should go and question James Maddok regarding his alleged involvement in this unsavoury and most unfortunate affair.

That evening, while still some distance from the Maddok house, the delegation was halted dead in its tracks by the sounds of the most blood chilling shrieks coming from the direction of the bungalow. The windows were ablaze with light from within, and fantastically animated shadows could be seen dancing and darting about in a frenzied fashion.

All this continued for long minutes while the delegation remained mesmerized into immobility. Then, suddenly, all fell deathly silent. It was a silence that was almost palpable. The memory of old Andrew Maddok's fate flooded suddenly to everyone's mind and they rushed the remaining distance to the house as one.

Deja vu best described the feelings of the group after they burst through the barred door and beheld what greeted them on the inside. James Arthur Maddok had indeed met with the same fate as his great uncle Andrew.

As the delegation stood transfixed in horror, old Ben methodically struck nine precisely spaced tones . . .

CHAPTER V

Charles Maddok stepped quietly into the study. His son, Kristian, sat in the broad window seat gazing out onto the expanse of well manicured lawn and newly budding rose garden. Kristian still held his uncle's last letter to him and the solicitor's copy of the last will and testament of James Arthur Maddok. Kristian had made up his mind, but was pondering on how best to break the news of his decision to his parents—and especially to his father.

Charles' footfalls had been hushed by the thick Persian carpets, but a creaking floor board had alerted Kristian to his father's presence.

"Oh, hello father," Kristian said abstractedly.

"Your mother and I have been awaiting your decision. We leave for France at the week's end and need to know if you will be accompanying us," Charles said, trying to keep his voice sounding normal and matter-of-fact.

Kristian turned to his father and looked into his suddenly tired face. His Maddok grey eyes, illuminated by the sunlight flooding into the room, had lost their own natural luminance ever since he had heard of his younger brother's hideous death; and also because of the foreknowledge of what his son's decision in this matter would most likely be.

Kristian had come to know and love his uncle James very well, and had greatly admired his independent spirit. A bond had grown between them that was, in some respects, stronger than the bond with his own parents. He had loved his uncle dearly and meant to unravel the mystery woven around his deeply disturbing death.

"No, father," Kristian said almost mechanically, "I will be going north to take up my inheritance. It will only be for a few months at most, I promise. I shall see you and mother back here before year's end."

Charles breathed a deep sigh of resignation, turned and left his son, his only son, to the view of his beloved rose garden. He secretly wished that he could do more himself and was therefore very proud, if not a little envious, of his son for his determination.

Kristian was, after all, past the age of majority and intelligent. Perhaps he would be the Maddok to bring these—these strange anomalies within the Maddok family to a definitive end . . .

Later, as his coach jostled and bumped its way along a rutted country road, Kristian stared at nothing in particular through the coach window and into the inky blackness of the starless night. He suddenly became aware of the reflection of his face staring back at him from the window pane. It startled him that he seemingly looked so hollow-eyed—almost cadaverous. He was very tired from the three days on the road, but he did not feel as bad as he apparently looked. It wouldn't be much longer now, though. The coachman had said that they should arrive at the village by about the next midday. Kristian pulled his travel rug close about him and tried to sleep.

He awoke with a jolt as the coach slewed to a halt in front of the livery stable cum way station of the little village. It was a bright day, but the road was still slick and sloppy from an early summer cloud burst the night before. As Kristian stepped gingerly down from the coach, he saw that a small carriage awaited his arrival, as arranged.

Save for the carriage driver, the rest of the street was devoid of any sign of other villagers; yet he felt as though he was being watched. He had anticipated spending a night at a village inn to rest and freshen up, but a feeling of discomfiture overtook him now and he decided to make straight for the Maddok house.

The coachman silently off-loaded his luggage, said a few murmured words to the carriage driver, then remounted the coach and was off. Kristian loaded his own luggage, as the carriage driver sullenly maintained his seat. An unnecessarily speedy and awkwardly silent ride ensued. Then, once at the house, Kristian off-loaded by himself. As he turned to pay, the driver merely wheeled the carriage about and proceeded back down towards the village without a word. Thus was the welcome to his new home.

The house was surprizingly tidy and clean. There was not the slightest hint at all of the last drama that had so gruesomely been played out.

Kristian set about his unpacking and putting his belongings in order. Just as he was finishing, the old grandfather clock struck three times. As he perfunctorily examined it, he noticed that it was almost fully wound. He was mulling this over when there was a knock at the door. A delicate, almost timid knock, he felt.

Emiline Herrik stood uncertainly on the stone slab at the door as it was opened to her by a tall, handsome man, perhaps in his early twenties. She smiled warmly up at him and introduced herself.

"Good afternoon, sir," she said in that north-country dialect that Kristian found so soft and musical. "I am Emiline Herrik. Welcome to our village." With that, she held out a wicker tray, the content of which was covered with crisp, clean, white linen.

"It's a meat pie, sir. I know that you must be hungry after your long journey, and there won't be any food in the house." She had also brought a ewer of fresh goat's milk. Kristian thanked her, relieved her of her burdens and invited her into the house. They settled onto chairs at opposite ends of the kitchen table and she accepted his offer of a glass of milk, but declined a slice of the meat pie.

Kristian inobtrusively studied this kindly village woman and decided that he very much liked what he saw. She had a youthful beauty that belied her age. Her eyes, the deep green of the seas, were large and intelligent—and something indefinably more. Shiny auburn hair was coiled up in a plaited bun on either side of head and accentuated the delicate bone structure of her face. The rather large, sensuous lips bespoke of a generous nature—and again, something more. Cleavage of an ample bosom showed through the diaphanous material of the blouse she wore beneath her pinafore dress.

He suddenly became aware that she had been telling him of herself and the relationship that she and her family had enjoyed with his uncle James. She hoped, she was saying, that they could be friends and that he would accept an invitation to supper some evening. He eagerly accepted the proffered friendship and the supper invitation. He just knew that he had to see more of this lovely, charming woman.

On the following evening Kristian found himself in the company of the Herrik family. Their home proved to be cozy and comfortable. A mouthwatering meal nestled itself deliciously in his stomach. It had been an altogether enjoyable evening. Emiline's family was truly charming. He had been readily accepted and had gotten along famously, even with her daughters.

After a time, the children had excused themselves and filed away to their beds. Kristian and Emiline were left to chat over cups of coffee and deliciously spiced biscuits. She was indeed an interesting and charming woman.

Far too soon the time to depart had arrived. As she walked him to the door and out into the night, she had slipped her arm through his. It felt so natural and right somehow. Then, as he turned to face her and thank her for the wonderful evening, she reached up and kissed him and thanked him for coming. Before he could respond, she was gone.

The warm pressure of her lips on his seemed to remain for the entire trip back to his house. That night he fell asleep with the sweet smell of her still tantalizingly with him.

The next several days were uneventful. Kristian busied himself by stocking his larder during the day, and taking long walks among the hills in the evenings. Game was plentiful and the fishing excellent. Still, he could not get the evening with Emiline out of his mind.

In his mind's eye he could see her smiling eyes and warm, sensuous mouth. He could almost hear her bubbling, musical laughter in the breeze through the leaves or the riffle of water in a brook. His nights were spent in dreams of this beguiling creature. He knew that he must see her again—soon.

CHAPTER VI

The village came alive with laughter and chatter and general good humour. The streets, shops and houses sported decorations of gaily coloured streamers and banners. The main street was alight with coloured lensed oil lamps. Shops and businesses would close early this day so that proprietors and clerks could be with their families. The villagers took their holidays and celebrations very much to heart, and Midsummer's Day was no exception.

Midsummer's Day had been, since time immemorial, a celebration of thanks for the good fortunes of the year, and thanks for an upcoming bountiful harvest. From darker times, it had been merely a show of gaiety and noisy revelry for the express purpose of dispelling evil, and discouraging demons from performing their usual deeds of havoc. While the young enjoyed the festivities as a welcome departure from the daily tedium of work, the elderly still clung to most of the ancient notions.

Kristian Maddok was in the village taking in the local charm of the occasion, when he suddenly felt—no, *knew* that he must be with the Herriks—with *Emiline* this day. As he strode purposefully to her house, he saw her standing at her door, waiting. Had she somehow been expecting him? She smiled enigmatically in silent greeting, took him by the hand and led him inside. He shrugged off an inexplicably uneasy feeling. It was probably only that he did not like to be anticipated, he thought.

It was then that he noticed a curious, heavy, copper bracelet pushed up her arm almost to the elbow. It was not the sort of personal adornment he would have expected to see on such a feminine arm. And what were those roughly hewn stones fastened around its surface? His musings were suddenly interrupted by the realization of his surroundings.

Emiline's bedroom was ablaze with light from innumerable candles—all of them black; truly a bewildering sight. Before he could recover from this bizarre sight, she had slipped her arms about his neck, brought his face to hers and kissed him so passionately, so heatedly that the room swam in a surreal sea of sensation. Suddenly his will was no longer his own.

A frenzied flurry of activity ensued, and then they were naked. He was aware now only of their bodies intertwining, writhing, becoming one. The mind hummed; the senses soared. Pleasure followed; pleasure so intense that it bordered on pain.

From somewhere seemingly very distant and yet somehow from within, came wordless murmurings. These murmurings seemed to undulate, to pulsate—like the very pulse of life itself—ever more rapidly. The meaningless murmurings grew in volume and intensity; grew towards a climax, until there was a thunderous, shouted:

"Maddok is mine!"

—And then complete, crushing silence and utter blackness; deep, engulfing blackness.

Truly a trap of sorts, but from whence deliverance—a possibility for ultimate escape . . .

CHAPTER VII

He wrote now with half frozen fingers, but a mind molten with words, ideas, scenes, episodes; and there was not nearly enough time. Time, that avaricious thief of all things—would it now and as well rob him of his final achievement?

He sat in the navigator's seat of the shattered cockpit with shattered and gangrenous legs, and peered through frost encrusted eyelashes at the approaching figures, grey and hazy in the frigid mountain mist.

They had crashed, how long ago, on this desolate Himalayan mountainside. Had it truly only been weeks? It seemed infinitely longer. All he knew for certain was that with their food supply completely exhausted, drawn lots had slowly, inexorably diminished the number of survivors. The losers (or were they ultimately winners?) were left to the near ravenous appetites of those who would hopefully survive to escape the same fate by somehow being rescued.

Occasionally someone would expire more or less naturally, and the next in line would be spared for a day or two, or maybe three.

The first to have succumbed to this fate had been an odd old gentleman: Andrew—something. Then his son, James (or had it been his grandson) had followed—how long ago? Now, it would soon be his turn.

He wrote more feverishly now, for the heat of his fevered mind was the only warmth afforded him. He must leave something of himself for—posterity? After all, there would soon be very little left of him physically.

He glanced bleakly around the broken, frost encrusted cockpit and his glance fell upon the cracked face of the craft's chronometer. The hands stood, now eternally frozen, at two minutes of eight. Old Ben would be striking the hour soon. So much to be done—so little time.

They were at the hatch now, beckoning voicelessly. He painfully scrawled a few more lines before their hands were upon him; gently lifting him from the seat; leading him to his destiny. It was mealtime . . .

Farewell to the Maddoks; farewell to the Herriks; farewell to the warm, close little village that might have been Shangri-la. It had all been just a brief escape. The ultimate escape was now at hand.

PART III

STRANGEWATER

Powers of Darkness

Cast thy spell;

Weave a web

As deep as Hell.

Into that web

Her soul shall plumb.

Harken now!

The Mistress doth come.

CHAPTER I

The day dawned, as days do; but this day there was only faint evidence of the sun as it shone bleakly through a thick pudding of cloud. The day began heavily, as so often before, like the dawning consciousness of Priscilla Strangewater, while she stirred from a troubled slumber.

Many times the dream had oozed from her subconscious to trouble her nocturnal trips of fancy. Many times she had heard her father's voice pleadingly try to communicate; but what was uttered were only inarticulations so unintelligible as to make comprehension virtually impossible. The inflections and tone were clear enough, as was an impression of his surroundings; but as to the meaning, the sense of it all, that evaded understanding.

His surroundings seemed frigid and misty in aspect. A sense of freezing numbness with an underlying physical pain kept surfacing. Whatever or wherever the strange and unfamiliar surroundings were, they seemed frost encrusted and uncomfortable in the extreme.

J. Clifton Strangewater III had been on a flight to Calcutta for a surveying mission when his aircraft had presumably iced up and gone down with seventeen crew and passengers somewhere in the lofty Himalayan range. Quite naturally, immediate rescue and retrieval had been virtually impossible, and nothing could be done but to wait for an accidental sighting. Even with a positive sighting, there could be only dim hope of retrieving bodies and rescuing survivors due to the extreme terrain.

The disappearance of her father's aeroplane had coincided with Priscilla's twenty-fifth birthday. Not that birthdays had held any charm or sense of excitement for her since her mother had died shortly before her first birthday; but this one had turned out to be particularly disheartening.

Medrik, her father's manservant, had tried, in his stiff and awkward way, to console her. Whether the consolation offered was for her father's accident or for her birthday, and the fact that she was still a spinster, was, however, not made entirely clear. At any rate, she appreciated the effort, which she was certain was made with the best of intentions.

It was at about this time that she had taken to walking the short distance into the town on her own. On one of these occasions, while wandering aimlessly and lost in thought, she had been abruptly halted, as though by some external but unseen force, before an old curio shop of sorts. Looking bewilderedly about, she saw no one; and to her recollection she had never been in this part of the town before.

She glanced up at the small, warped and much weathered marquee over the door, and made out the name of Maddok's Muse. Immediately an electrified, prickling sensation crept up the back of her neck and scalp. Maddok!—*Maddok*! Her subconscious mind seemed to know that name, but that knowledge only tickled and niggled at the outer reaches of her consciousness. Finally she shrugged off the effort at recognition and entered the shop.

Later, she would not recall encountering anyone in the shop—proprietor or customer alike—or even what the shop's interior was like—except for a sense of musty gloom. However, when she emerged, as if from a dream, she found that she clutched a crudely wrapped little parcel.

She felt her spirits suddenly, somehow lifted, and as she walked briskly back to the Strangewater manor, there was an unaccustomed spring in her step. By the time she had arrived back at the manor, she was literally giddy with anticipation; much like she had been as a child on Christmas morning. She fairly flew to her rooms and, still clad in her mantle and hat, tore open her coarse little package.

She was, at first, taken aback by the parcel's content. Then, little by little she warmed to it. It was certainly not what she was accustomed to, nor was it to her particular taste. Then again she had never really taken enough interest in such things to develop a really personal taste in them. As she turned it slowly over and over in her hands and examined every minute detail of it, it was as though it began to exert an almost mesmeric influence over her.

Then the sun suddenly slid from behind a darkling cloud and, through a window next to which she stood, shone a ray directly onto its burnished copper surface making the six pentagonal lode stones stand out in stark contrast.

She slid the ancient bracelet over her hand and onto her wrist. Almost immediately a mild galvanic tingling sensation seemed to course up her arm and, from there, through her entire body. She had never felt so alive, so envigorated, so—so sensuous.

Young, but rather spinsterish, Priscilla Strangewater whom so little of life had ever touched; to whom nothing exciting in life had ever happened, was now suddenly, inexplicably filled with the full sense and awareness of womanhood. She had never questioned anything about or in her life; not even who her father's manservant, Medrik, was or where he had come from. Now, all at once, inexplicably, Medrik's identity and past seemed of intense interest. It was as though her mother's untimely death at such an early age had submerged Priscilla in a state of shock and ennui from which, only now, was she resurfacing.

Medrik was a strange, silent man of an indeterminate age and ancestry. He had a faint accent that bespoke of mid-European roots, but nothing definite. He was only slightly taller than Priscilla, and age notwithstanding, had a youthful musculature and grace that Priscilla had only just begun to notice.

Medrik doubled as gardener for the Maddok manor's grounds and, when working out of doors on warm, sunny days, would strip to the waist to bend to his tasks. Priscilla began noticing more and more about this mysterious man; for now he had begun to intrigue her. Intrigue her—and something more.

Medrik had not been in the habit of accompanying Priscilla's father on any of his business trips. He and Mr. Strangewater had long since come to an understanding that Medrik would remain at the manor, as he had put it: "to look after things on the home front".

The entire complement of household staff, with the exception of Medrik and Rowena, the cook/housekeeper, had, however, been released for the summer. Unused rooms had been draped and closed up, and the manor had taken on a quiet, somewhat sombre atmosphere. This had suited Priscilla's temperament at the outset, but now she became restless and not a little bored with the lack of bustle and sounds of humanity.

To assuage her boredom, on one occasion in the town, she had a hairdresser change her rather plain coiffure to something more appealing and modern. On subsequent occasions, she would buy some colourful millinery creation, or new shoes—the higher-heeled fashion as opposed to the dowdy, flat-heeled style that she had been accustomed to; a few new dresses, more flouncy, colourful and feminine in fashion, to replace her usual plain and dreary matron-like garb.

On one of these trips she had even discovered the exciting world of alternative lingerie from Paris. It was a strangely tittilating discovery, to be sure. She had always thought of undergarments and sleepwear as basically utilitarian in nature, but there was definitely a certain sensuous delight in merely wearing some of these new-found marvels.

In between times she would take the air in the gardens of the manor. On these occasions she would seem to gravitate to wherever Medrik happened to be working. Sometimes she would just stand and watch him. Othertimes she would engage him in a little conversation. For his part, it was very little conversation indeed, but she didn't seem to mind in the least. Little by little she began to find out more about him.

There had been some scandal regarding his birth; some scandal aside from the fact that he had been conceived as a result of an illegitimate union between a country widow and a young city gentleman, who had been some years her junior. The young gentleman had subsequently, apparently, taken a seizure and lain in a coma until Medrik's birth. Then, quite mysteriously, he had simply vanished without a trace.

Medrik had pondered aloud that if reincarnation was possible, then he may well be the reincarnation of his own father. Priscilla did not see the humour in such a notion, if, in fact, humour was intended. As a matter of fact, she regarded it as an entirely strange and disquieting concept. It was disquieting, she reasoned, because however tenuous the possibility of Medrik being right was, the possibility might be present nonetheless.

CHAPTER II

Throughout the ill-ventilated and equally ill-lit, capacious cellar of the Strangewater manor, hung the cloying pall of damp decay. This damp decay mingled with the animal odour of a long- confined being. Through the musty stillness, stirrings and sub- human grunts and grumblings were occasionally punctuated by equally sub-human snarls and shrieks. These sounds echoed eerily throughout the dim subterranean basement without ever penetrating the heavily acousticised ceiling.

Across one end of the cellar, whence the sounds emanated, stood a sturdy wall of iron bars—floor to ceiling, wall to wall and some six to eight feet from the end wall. Therein paced the tatter shrouded figure of what, from a distance, one could be forgiven for not recognizing as a woman. She had long and tangled ebon hair; the whole of which was caked with filth and alive with vermin. Through this filth and vermin, however, radiated a voluptuousness and obvious, though evil, beauty rarely witnessed in human form or face.

From the far end of the basement came a loud, metallic clack, and then the ponderous grating of a heavy door being swung open upon ancient, rusting hinges. Through the doorway came a man of average height and build; and although of indeterminate age, had a youthful musculature and walked with an easy grace. In his hands he bore an enormous serving tray upon which sat a large bowl of steaming, pungent broth, a half loaf of coarse, black bread and a ewer of buttermilk.

The pacings of the caged creature halted. The sounds she made were reduced to low, throaty rumblings as she eyed the approaching figure with rapt interest and began salivating prodigiously.

"There now," intoned Medrik, "I realize it is past your mealtime, but I have some good news, as well."

At this, the creature shifted her rapt attention from the food tray to the face of the approaching figure and tried to penetrate the inscrutability of that face.

Upon reaching the wall of bars, he knelt and passed the bowl and half loaf through a low opening at the bottom, and the ewer between the vertical bars. While he still knelt, she approached the bars and extended through them a naked and filthy foot, the toes of which had sprouted long, curved nails. Medrik bent reverently forward and lovingly pressed his lips to the proffered appendage. She smiled down at him in a grimly benevolent fashion as he said,

"Your humble servant, oh daughter of Gog."

Then, in a coarse, gravelly voice, she said, "You are forgiven for your tardiness, my faithful. Tell me of your good news while I eat and drink. Then, afterwards, I may tell you some good news of my own."

With that, she tore the half loaf asunder and began sopping up the broth.

Medrik related to her the gradual changes taking place with Priscilla; her awakening interest in him and, with particular and open delight, related Priscilla's discovery of the bracelet—the bracelet of Gog.

At this last bit of intelligence, the creature rumbled in obvious satisfaction. But when it was disclosed where the ancient bracelet had been found—the name of the curio shop—she momentarily halted her feeding and looked up with brows knitted in some perplexity. Then she merely grunted and returned to her meal with renewed gusto.

Upon completion of the meal, she leaned back on her heels and emitted a loud, grating belch which reverberated for some time around the subterranean chamber. This was followed with a volley of bawdy, raucous laughter until tears coursed trails through the accumulated grime on her cheeks.

Abruptly the mirth vanished and she rumbled, "Now, Medrik my faithful, observe what I can do."

With that, she rose from her squatted position and stood in the centre of her enclosure, with legs slightly parted, arms spread wide and head thrown back. Presently she began glowing with a faint, white light. A fine, greenish mist began swirling around her, and her face, her entire being seemed to transmute.

For long seconds Medrik was mesmerized by the apparent transformation. Then he gasped and stepped back startled, as he realized that what he was looking at—*whom* he was looking at was— *Priscilla.*

The creature dropped her arms, jerked her head upright and the vision abruptly disappeared. She threw her head back and cackled shrilly at the expression of amazement on Medrik's strickened face.

"So, you see, my faithful, it begins at last," she trilled to the slowly recovering Medrik. "Now you know what you must do; and soon," she said in a suddenly sonorous tone.

"Yes, yes, of course," Medrik gasped. "I believe she is almost ready. It will be done as you command, oh eternal, glorious daughter of Gog."

He again fell to his knees as the creature extended her other foot for his adoring homage. After he had gathered the bowl and ewer, he left the chamber trembling with pent up excitement. Soon she would be all powerful and truly eternal, and she would remember and reward the one who had made it all possible.

Medrik's mind cast back to the time when, with Priscilla's mother, his own daughter, he had sired this daughter on behalf of the Lord of Gog. Of course it had been necessary that Priscilla's mother be sacrificed; but an eternity of power—awesome power—was worth any sacrifice. This power would be his reward. Hadn't he dedicated and sacrificed most of his life to this end? So it would be a most just reward.

He recalled the story of his great uncle, James Maddok, who had been too weak, or too ignorant, or both to do what was necessary. An involuntary shudder surged through him as he recalled that ancestor's fate.

Priscilla was now intrigued and captivated enough to be quite easily seduced. Now that she wore that bracelet almost constantly, the union could proceed during this her greatest suseptability. Their carnal coupling was necessary, of course, to create that suseptability. Once Priscilla and Morgwyna, the daughter of Gog, were united as one single entity, Medrik's rewards would be assured

The anticipation was almost overwhelming for Medrik, but he must proceed with the utmost caution. The slightest problem now could result in his complete undoing.

It had been fortuitous, indeed, when Priscilla's father had presumeably perished in the aeroplane crash. He may have proven to be a difficult obstacle. It had been difficult enough when Priscilla's mother had *mysteriously* become pregnant so soon after Priscilla's birth.

CHAPTER III

Priscilla awoke suddenly with a sense of mild panic. She had experienced a strange dream that, although she could not recall the details of, had left her with the strangest sensation—a sensation of—of evaporating into nothingness.

She sprang from her bed and hurried to stand before her full length cheval-glass. Her reflected image seemed to have a faint, pearlescent glow, which, as she stood transfixed, faded slowly back to her skin's natural hue. After a moment she shook herself out of her befuddled reverie and glanced to the window for a possible explanation. She could see that the near full moon had just slid behind a cloud. Thus, she satisfied herself that it must have been the moon's rays that had lent her such a pearly visage—and yet! Yet, what of the sensation? It had seemed so real.

"Only a vivid dream," she grudgingly allowed—and yet! "Enough! Back to bed with you," she chided herself. And so again to bed, and to sleep, albeit not a restful sleep.

The morning dawned so beautifully that the gloriously fresh aspect of everything almost made Priscilla forget the disturbing event of the night before—almost. Try as she might, she could not dispell a feeling of—of foreboding. But why foreboding? It was only a silly dream—a nightmare of sorts—wasn't it?

Perhaps this ridiculous feeling could be dispelled by some diversion with Medrik. Perhaps a chat and a walk in the gardens.

Medrik, however, was nowhere to be found. The housekeeper/cook, Rowena, when questioned as to his whereabouts, hesitatingly offered that she had seen him walking in the direction of the town at about dawn. Somewhat puzzled by this halting revelation, but still seeking diversion, Priscilla decided that a walk into the town in the fresh, warm air might be just what she needed.

After some time spent meandering through the streets of the quainter quarter, she suddenly recognized the street, or rather the lane, in which stood that odd little shop. What was it called? Maddok's Muse! At the recollection of the name of Maddok, the seeming recognition of it again niggled at the outer reaches of her consciousness—just out of reach, however.

As she stepped into the lane, fully intending to go again to that shop, she stopped short. There was Medrik, just exiting the shop. He carried, in the crook of one arm, two small packages. Involuntarily she sidestepped into the dim recess of a deep doorway. As Medrik passed, unaware of Priscilla's presence, he was quietly humming a tune and smiling enigmatically to himself.

She was surprized; and then, somehow not surprized in the least, that Medrik should be aware of the existence of that little shop. They, he and the shop, seemed somehow akin to each other.

After he had passed into the adjoining street, Priscilla continued on towards Maddok's Muse. Upon arriving, however, she was puzzled to find that the door was locked and shuttered. As it could not be much later than mid-morning, she wondered at the shop being closed. It had obviously been open only moments before, and yet now it was closed. It was almost as though it had been open only for Medrik, given the singular lack of pedestrian traffic in the lane.

Of course, Priscilla would never have dreamt, nor had reason to believe, that Medrik was, in fact, the proprietor. Nor could she have known that Maddok's Muse had been passed down to Medrik from a distant relative by the name of Andrew Maddok. Had she been privy to this knowledge, she may have been able to perceive the labyrinthine tapestry into which she had been so inextricably woven; and what fate may well have in store for her.

As it was, her powers of deduction, never very strongly developed, were now virtually non-existent. Any good that may have come from even keenly tuned powers of deduction at this point, would merely have been ex post facto, and therefore effectively nullified.

Later, after luncheoning at a prosaic little cafe, and returning home, Priscilla found that Rowena had been called away to tend to her ailing mother. The cook/housekeeper would apparently be required to attend her mother through the night. Assurances had been made, however, that she would return in time to prepare breakfast on the following morning. Priscilla thought the arrangement inconvenient, if not a little odd, but shrugged it off and thought no more of it. But what then of the evening meal?

Priscilla had never so much as prepared a sandwich, not to mention an evening meal, albeit for one—or rather two. There was Medrik to consider. She was much relieved therefore when Medrik persuaded her that his culinary abilities were more than up to the task.

They dined together that evening, at Priscilla's insistence. She saw little sense in Medrik serving her in the dining room, and then going back to the kitchen to feed himself.

Medrik was as good as his word. The meal was superb—if a little heady. The sauces were especially delightful—from old country recipes, he informed her. Even the conversation was delightful, and far more spontaneous on Medrik's part than was his wont.

He seemed to be in a particularly congenial mood, and it seemed to be infectious. At one point, after the meal, and the wine, they even danced together to the music from some of her mother's old gramaphone records.

As they whirled to the music, Priscilla seemed to drift into another world—a dream world where the sensuous beat of the music became all-enveloping. She seemed to float in a cloud of sensual awareness—awareness of the latent needs of a woman now pulsating to the surface. The aphrodisiac herbs, with which Medrik had liberally laced Priscilla's meal, were having their effect.

CHAPTER IV

In the cellar below, awareness was also present. Morgwyna swayed lithely and hummed an ancient chant. She could feel the moment nearing—a moment that she had awaited in this vermin- ridden pest-hole for almost a quarter of a century. She had paid this prodigious price all in preparation for what would soon be hers—immortality and fearsome powers.

Her loins undulated and twitched as she began to glow in pearlescent light. As a greenish mist began swirling, first at her feet, then slowly upward, she could almost feel Medrik's manhood moving within her. A sense of power is also a strong aphrodisiac.

Meanwhile, Priscilla sank ever deeper in a sea of unparalleled delight, as from the distant depths a greenish mist with a pearlescent core rose to meet her.

Such a bounty of sensual joy had never even been vaguely imagined in her closeted, morose little life. Now she felt as though she could not live without it.

Ever closer drifted the greenish mist. Priscilla, now aware of it, welcomed it; believing, in her libidinous torpor, that it must contain even greater bliss.

All the while, Medrik's ragged breathing quickened and became increasingly laboured. The years of grovelling servitude and bestial deeds would soon reap their rewards for him. He could sense culmination fast approaching.

Nearer and nearer came the swirling, greenish mist with its glowing, pulsating, pearlescent nucleus. Priscilla and Morgwyna now felt each other's growing ecstacy—pleasure, bordering on pain.

Pain—*pain*! Somewhere there *was* pain!

The universe exploded in searing light. A long, drawn scream ensued from somewhere—from everywhere. Then deep, engulfing, soul numbing blackness.

CHAPTER V

Frigid mists swirled around the shattered and frost encrusted remains of an air craft on a snow shrouded mountain side in the lofty Himalayan range. The mists and snow swirled and scudded as the first of a rescue party sighted its quarry.

Elation quickly faded to apprehension as shouted greetings and inquiries elicited no response but the moaning of the mountain winds. Apprehension coalesced into realization as the first human remains were discovered.

Cannibalism in such circumstances, though hideous to contemplate, was not uncommon, nor difficult to comprehend given the painful alternative.

What had become of the remaining passenger or passengers was never discovered. Perhaps one of the myriad of bottomless crevasses or a snowslide had claimed whomever remained. The cockpit crew had apparently and mercifully been killed outright.

Aside from the captain's flight log and cargo and passenger manifests, the only other written record found was a journal of sorts; a seemingly cryptic account by a passenger named J. Clifton Strangewater III. It was assigned as the probable ravings of a man demented by pain and the approach of death.

The Strangewater journal contained, for the greater part, a dissertation on the generations of a family by the name of Maddok. With the good and the evil, it detailed the descent of that family replete with its ultimate goal, and Strangewater's unaccountable powerlessness to foil the final realization of that goal.

The final entry read: "Medrik Maddok, with his congenital heart defect, inherited through generations of incest, must always remain celebate, or surely die. Luck will not be with him a *second* time. May the Fates deal kindly with my child. I had always meant to warn her. It is my fondest hope that in time she may forgive me."

Weeks later, as Priscilla read her father's journal, she wept with complete comprehension.

Maddok Genealogy

Morgwyn (Mad Dog) Maddok—Gwythlyn The Good

/   /   /   /   /   /   /   \ \ \

Mardrak Morgyn Mordred Medryk Gwendolyn Katrina Letiea Teulyna and three still births

(illigitimate unions)

Morgwyn Maddok—Gwendolyn—Katrina—Letiea

/   \ \ \ \ \

Agwelyn and six unrecorded births

/ / / / /

\ \ \ \ \ \

(illigitimate union)   / / / / / /

Morwyn Maddok—Agwelyn Maddok   \ \ \ \ \ \

/ /   / / / / / /

two unrecorded births   \ \ \ \ \ \

\ \   / / / / / /

/ /   \ \ \ \ \ \

\ \   / / / / / /

The Lost Generations

/   \

\   /

/   \

(illigitimate union)

Garyth Maddock—Agnetha Gorm   Arthur Angus Maddok—Karyn Stek

/   /

Morgan Maddok—Gwynyth Armwyn   Emiline Maddok—Kort Herrik

/   \   /   /   /   \   \

Charles   (still birth) James   Kristine Tomas Karl Emilia Edwyna

/   \   /

\   /   \

/   (illigitimate union)

\   /

/   (died at birth)

\—Sylvia Kroub

/

\   (illigitimate union)

Kristian—Emiline Herrik (Maddok)

/

Medrik Maddok—(unnamed woman)

\   (illigitimate union)

J. Clifton Strangewater—Kristina Maddok   Medrik Maddok—Kristina Strangewater

/   /

Priscilla Strangewater   Morgwyna Maddok

(Mistress of Gog)

THE BATH TUB

Paula Haimes' latest acquisition for her and Ben's Edwardian fixer-upper stood, uncrated and in all its splendour, in the beige and white tiled foyer. It was, the quaint little antique dealer had said, late Victorian, British. Late Victorian or not, it was marvelously unique. Exactly how unique, Paula was yet to find out.

It was a ball and claw footed bath tub with, not four, but six feet. Bronze feet, they were. Another unnusual feature, which had immediately caught Paula's eye, had been the extra large overflow outlet. It had grinned at her in six barred opulence from under the gleaming set of bronze spiggot and faucets. Paula had grinned back and fallen in love.

Paula and Ben Haimes had acquired this house in a bequest from a distant aunt of Ben's, coincidentally on their wedding anniversary; their thirteenth wedding anniversary. While Ben had had some serious reservations concerning the condition of the old house, Paula, always one to have instant black or white reactions to things, had taken to it instantly.

She had appealed to Ben's dislike of traffic and long commutes by pointing out that the house was situated no more than a fifteen minute drive from his work place. And that, with just the money he'd save in not having the long commute, they would be able to pay for even major renovations in no more than five years time.

Eventually, in the face of such overwhelming, if unusual logic so deftly applied by Paula, Ben had allowed himself to be swayed, and had stayed his hand from putting the place up for sale as was.

"Oh, you won't be sorry, Benny." (He hated it when she called him *Benny*; she thought he loved it as an endearment.) "We should be able to do a lot of the renovations ourselves—you're so handy at these things—and won't it be such fun," Paula had gushed. "We can put an extra bathroom in the basement, and finish the basement to create a place for entertaining and to retreat to in the summer's heat," she had bubbled.

"Mmm-hmm," Ben had said, and groaned inwardly, having some considerable doubts about how much *fun* it would really be.

Ben had grown up with parents who were continually on the move from one fixer-upper to yet another. Just when a place became comfortably liveable and something not to be ashamed of coming home to, they would put it on the market, then buy another, and the process would begin again. He had become totally fed up with it by the time he was about ten or twelve.

Paula, on the other hand, had grown up with parents that had lived in the same house since before she had been born, and still did live there—forty-two years and counting. So Paula was always ready for a new adventure in accommodation. Ben had hoped that after living in four different apartments (fixer-uppers all) in twelve years, she might have outgrown her quest for *adventure*. But apparently not.

###

In his spare time and on weekends, Ben had roughed out the plumbing for the basement bathroom and a "place for entertaining" and "to retreat to in the summer's heat". He had also removed and reinstalled the closet shower from the upstairs bathroom to make room for Paula's monster, six legged, "late Victorian" bath tub with the toothy, grinning overflow outlet. Quite an *evil*, toothy grin he had thought to himself. It kind of reminded him of the grin on the face of a jack-o-lantern. Oh well, it was Paula's love; he preferred showers, himself.

Paula could hardly wait for the bath tub to be installed for her first bath. She was actually in it, giving it a scrub, while Ben was putting the finishing touches on connecting the plumbing.

"Benny," she said, "Did you notice that the overflow grill bars actually do look like teeth?"

"Umm-hmm," he mumbled from somewhere between the wall and the head of the tub.

"Yah! They're tapered towards the bottom just like some kind of fangs. Isn't that extraordinary?"

"Hmmph," came a muffled reply; and then a painful thump and, "Oww, jeezus, shit!"

"Oh, Ben!" she gasped, "I do hope you haven't chipped the enamel. Do try and be more careful, sweetheart."

"I'll try not to bleed on the bloody thing," he grated between clenched teeth. "Would you see if you could find me a bandaid. I seem to have thoughtlessly hammered a knuckle."

"Of course, dear. But there's no need to take that tone," she chided. "Civility doesn't cost a thing."

Immediately after the tub was completely installed and fully operational, Paula began filling it in preparation for a 'test run' as she called it. While she did that, Ben took himself off to have a beer or six and try and calm himself.

The bath tub was just wonderful; it seemed to *fit* so well somehow. And it also seemed to keep the water warm for longer than usual. The tub's surface seemed pliant, almost like an upholstered surface. Paula luxuriated in its comfort; in its—its *caress*. Yes, it was almost like a caress, Paula thought.

"Oh dear, now I'm waxing poetic about a bath tub," she said aloud and startled herself out of a semi-doze.

That's when she noticed them. No, it couldn't be, but yes, there they were—*eyes*. Two eyes peering at her from behind the overflow grill. Shiny, pale green eyes—pale green fading to yellow at their centres. Two eyes shimmering palidly in the dark recesses of the overflow pipe. Two eyes peering unblinkingly, hypnotically—.

Paula's piercing scream jarred Ben rudely back to full consciousness. He took the stairs two and three at a stride and arrived just in time to see Paula slithering over the side of the bath tub like an inebriated eel.

"Wha—what the hell is it, Paula?" he gasped after his unaccustomed show of athletics.

Paula jabbered for some minutes about eyes peering at her from beyond the overflow grill. Hideous, staring eyes watching her nakedness. Then slowly, as Ben held her, trying to comfort her, she began listening to herself. Listening and hearing how completely insane it all sounded. But she had seen something; she knew she had.

She shamefacedly looked up at Ben and asked him if he could look in through the overflow grill and see what he thought. Upon inspection, Ben soon discovered what it had been that Paula had mistaken for eyes. There were two inward protuberances in the casting of the brass overflow pipe to accommodate tapped holes from the outside. A pipe clamp was meant to be attached, with the aid of machine screws, for the purpose, he supposed, of securing the standpipe part of a shower attachment. The light shining through the grill, either directly or reflected from the water, in turn reflected off the protuberances and gave the impression of two shiny, staring eyes.

Paula gave an embarrassed little titter, once she could see it all for herself. She pecked Ben on the cheek and said, "You really are a clever fellow, Benny. I'm sorry if I startled you; but it really is kind of funny, don't you think."

"Yes, absolutely hilarious," he intoned, massaging a cramp in his calf. He gave her a kiss on the forehead and returned to his unfinished beer and crossword.

###

The bath tub incident slowly faded out of conscious memory, and daily life resumed a modicum of normalcy. The renovations continued, and after a few months the old *money pit*, as Ben had taken to calling the old house, finally became comfortably liveable.

For the first few baths that Paula had taken after *the incident*, she had still felt a little uneasy about the bath tub but soon chided herself out of it. A bath in it had, after all, a very comfortable and extraordinarily relaxing feel about it. And she had been a bit silly about the whole *eyes* thing, she thought.

To inaugurate the newly finished entertainment area (Paula hated the term: *rec. room*), they decided to invite some friends over for the evening. Just something simple and easy, Ben had advised. Paula, who never did anything by halves, spent the best part of the day preparing. When Ben came home and saw the results, he felt that he had been grossly amiss in not installing at least one three tier crystal chandelier.

The evening went swimmingly. Everyone had a guided tour through the refurbished old house (to many an "*ooh!*" and "*aah!*") and, according to Paula, simply adored the bath tub. Ben couldn't help but grin at that bit of intelligence. She really does love that tub; she's almost maternal towards it, he mused to himself.

"Next thing is she'll be feeding the damned thing," he giggled to himself, a little worse off for all the wine he'd consumed.

"What was that, sweetheart?" Paula said as she loaded the dishwasher.

"Nothing, hon." (Paula hated that term, it sounded so common). "I'm just going down for a shower. Be up in a little."

"Okay, Benny. I think I'll have a nice hot bath before I turn in. I'm still a little wound up and it'll relax me."

"Awright, sugar."

Paula thought *that* sounded common as well. She sometimes marvelled at how little of her culture had rubbed off on him in thirteen years of marriage. Oh well, there was time yet, she thought.

Ben thoroughly enjoyed his shower, singing an old Gordon Lightfoot ballad that he had enjoyed in his youth. Paula would probably have thought that was common, or at least uncultured, as well, he thought, and enjoyed it all the more.

He then went up to bed and was asleep within seconds of his head hitting the pillow. He dreamed of doing a road tour with Gordon Lightfoot, and playing a little backup guitar for him. He slept soundly and hardly moved a muscle the whole night.

When Ben awoke to Saturday morning sunshine streaming into his eyes, he immediately felt that something wasn't quite right. He donned his glasses and peered sleepily at his bedside clock. It was 8:05. Maybe a bit early for a *Saturday* morning; but what was wrong?

Then he noticed the unusual absence of soft snoring from Paula's bed. He glanced over in that direction, then shuffled over and lifted the covers on her bed. The soft snore wasn't the only thing absent. It seemed that Paula hadn't slept in the bed at all.

"Where the devil is she at this time in the morning? Ah, wait a minute; she's fallen asleep in that bloody bath tub, that's it. Well, it'll serve her right if she's all cramped up in cold bath water."

Ben sniggered to himself at the image that he conjured up: Quasimoto in a kimono.

"I guess I'd better go and wake her," he said. "I can just see how the rest of my day is going to go."

But he couldn't really see—not really.

Ben eased the bathroom door open and peered in. The bath tub was empty except for surprizingly still tepid, frothy water. As he was pondering where else she might be and reaching for the drain plug, his eyes were suddenly drawn to the overflow drain.

There, tangled in the toothy grin, was a clump of hair. It looked like Paula's hair—it *was* Paula's hair. He was sure of it.

"By god, I've heard of moulting," he said, "but this is ridiculous."

But he couldn't shake the feeling of unease. Then, as he reached for the hair, he heard the unmistakable sound of a low, grating belch echoing up through the overflow pipe, followed closely by the unmistakeable odour of—of *raw meat*.

"Raw meat! What the hell!" he croaked as he yanked the clump of hair loose from the overflow grill.

Attached to the hair was a bloody, ragged patch of scalp. His scream lasted beyond the scope of breath that he had for it. Then complete blackness. Blackness from which there was no returning.

The End

2026-2040
A NEW BEGINNING

It was a sweltering August afternoon when Morlen Quencis finally, irrevocably made up his mind that all work with little joy would not be *his* future.

As he took a break in the stuffy little accounts office, with sweat coursing tickling paths down his body, he glanced through the single, grimy, little window towards the cacophony emanating from the loading yard. Three dogs were taking their turns with a bitch in heat.

"Isn't that just like life," he thought, as two of the excited dogs tried to take their turns at the same time. "But, if you could just grab your turn first, what would it matter what came after—as long as you got what you wanted."

His father was a grain farmer, as his father before him had been, and so on into the dim recesses of the past. Well, moiling in the soil wasn't Morlen's idea of a fulfilling vocation. However, here he was grubbing away for a seed vendor for a pittance (and whatever he could *liberate* on the side).

Morlen had heard of a past time when a person with intelligence and drive could be and do anything he set his mind to, and when even a little money had some value. Although that was no longer the case, nor had it been for some time, perhaps his intelligence and drive could get him somewhere by other means. He would like to be able to do more for his mother. She, at least, had never taken him for granted.

His poor mother had married into a life of endless drudgery with a man of no imagination, drive, compassion, or scope beyond the bounds of farming.

His father was a man whose high point might be a day without hail or blowing dust or grasshoppers nibbling at his crop; a man whose painfully limited outlook on life virtually made his life a wasted experience, in Morlen's view. But his mother, whose enduring loveliness seemed lost on her husband, was a clever, intelligent and resourceful woman, whose only shortcoming seemed to have been her choice of a life's partner.

Vague notions about what to do next were beginning to coalesce into some form. Should deception and usery need to be employed in whatever *grand plan* he came up with, then so be it. However, the next two years would see changes in Morlen and his circumstances that even he couldn't have foreseen, much less planned. The time he had been born to would mould his *grand plan* far more effectively than any of his mental machinations.

###

The year was 2038. Twelve years had passed since the International Monetary Fund collapsed under the sheer weight of its own bureaucracy and the wild fluctuations of world currencies. Not even the mighty Euro-dollar had proven immune to the calamity. Twelve years had passed since the resultant socio-economic upheaval had begun; an upheaval unequalled in human memory.

A worldwide economic depression raged. General discontent had reached epidemic proportions. Then social unrest turned to unbridled violence, and no fewer than eleven heads-of-state had been assassinated within two years; with many more in dire peril of their lives.

Bartering for goods and services had generally replaced the purchase of them with virtually worthless currencies. All that most families had to barter with, however, were their own members. Thus, incidences of prostitution and indenturing (or virtual slavery) mushroomed. All the social enlightenments of previous times had evapourated like so much mist in a gale.

A sexually mature child could be indentured for up to five years in return for three months worth of food for a family of four; or a bicycle. Men and women may have to travel up to thirty miles to work, should they have been fortunate enough to have found any. Gasoline and diesel oil had long since risen in price to over fifteen dollars a litre. As a result, there were few indeed who could afford to operate a motor vehicle (much less own one). The United North American base labour rate of twenty dollars an hour, as set in 2020, was beyond laughable in the face of the situation that began only six short years later. Home ownership for many was a mere memory. A two bedroom bungalow on the seamy side of a major North American city would sell for upwards of three million dollars—or the indenturing of a pair of pretty twelve year old girls until such time as they were no longer either useful or pretty. The fortunate home owners were those who had been able to purchase prior to 2020—and keep up with the ever escalating property taxes.

The justice systems had collapsed, and crime prevention and policing of laws had all but ceased. What police there still were, had their time and resources taken up mostly with the protection of government officials—a daunting task in itself. Police mortality in major urban areas had rapidly risen to one in ten.

The health care systems had all but collapsed as well. The infant mortality rate among the working class and unemployed had risen to one in twenty-three worldwide. The chances of pregnant women, within these classes, delivering a live or viable child, or indeed surviving childbirth themselves, was one in fifteen.

The global unemployment rate had reached sixty-three percent, and of those who were employed, little more than one percent had been able to keep the same job for as long as three years. Such was the competition for gainful employment, that labour unions had ceased to exist by 2029.

Government sanctioned euthanasia had grudgingly been universally accepted by 2030. However, by 2038 more than twenty million people had been euthanized worldwide. Further to this was that the death penalty for capital crimes had been instituted in countries that had previously viewed it as immoral, and cruel and unusual punishment.

Since regular burial of human remains had been outlawed by 2031, the estimated hundred and twenty thousand crematoria worldwide were operating continuously, twenty-four hours per day, three hundred and sixty-five days per year.

The 2021 world census had pegged the global population at seven and a quarter billion. By 2038, however, it was estimated that that figure had dropped by almost one billion.

In short, whomever man had not killed for economic reasons, had died from various diseases or starvation, which in reality amounted to the same cause. In those times, if one had a miserable existence (and most did) but remained disease-free, then one was counted as fortunate indeed.

On March 31, 2026, Morlen Quencis, a seven pound and twelve ounce baby boy was born to Agnea and Quentin Quencis of Arlyn Flats in the south-central district of the state of Manitoba. The arrival of this child went largely uncelebrated, not to say unnoticed, by the people of this plebeian community. The state of the district's communal crops was infinitely higher on their general priorities list. That attitude, however, was to alter significantly in time to come.

As Morlen matured, a precocious intellect began developing, and being noticed by most; and as he matured, this intellect began being used in intemporate ways. Along with his intelligence, or perhaps as a result of it, he developed a charm to match. Consequently, the inappropriate use of it seemed ameliorated. "How clever!", "Wasn't that cute!", and the like seemed the commonest epithets concerning the actions and deeds of young Morlen Quencis.

Once, Morlen managed the trade of a neighbour's horse that had been pastured on his father's land, for a bicycle. The bicycle was used to travel the eight miles into town where he had found employment at a seed vendor's.

The farmer, whose horse had thus been bartered without his immediate knowledge, had subsequently been convinced through circuitous logic that not only was the bicycle worth more than the horse, but that the horse was beyond its serviceable years and was in fact a liability to him. Therefore Morlen had indeed performed an invaluable and selfless service. The farmer, never noted for great mental acuity, was so grateful that he allowed Morlen to keep the bicycle as payment for the great service thus rendered.—"Intelligent lad!"

During his year and a half employment with the seed vendor, Morlen had not only succeeded in putting the small company's financial books in order, a job that he, incidentally, had not been hired for, but also in smoothly and undetectably embezzling some three thousand dollars. All in all, not bad for a boy just approaching his twelfth year.—"Sharp as a tack, that boy!"

For his twelfth birthday, Morlen decided to indulge himself with something of an unique present. He arranged, with the grudging approval of his parents, to indenture himself to a retired judge for a small stipend and the services of a fourteen year old girl who lived with the judge and his housekeeper. The girl, although pretty and physically well developed, was not the brightest of individuals. However, Morlen had decided that it was high time that he became a man, in the carnal sense at least.—"What a clever boy!"

Retired circuit court judge, Alexander Cartwyth, had been promising himself for years to begin his memoirs. When a clearly intelligent boy from outside of town had offered his services as a general go-for and companion for what amounted to an unusual, if not an intriguing settlement, he decided to take the bull by the horns. Besides, he thought the boy might keep that witless girl out of his hair. He had only taken her on as a favour to an old friend, who could no longer cope with her or afford to keep her.

He had met Morlen while doing a bit of contract work for a small seed vendoring firm in Arlyn Flats. The boy had shown a remarkable acumen in accounting and general business matters, and was generally agreeable and interesting company.

The judge arranged to allow the two of them the run of an upstairs suite that included a spacious bedroom with twin beds and an ensuite bathroom. The boy duly arrived on his bicycle and ensconced his few meagre belongings in what was to become his new home for the next two years.

Morlen was well pleased with his new situation. The work would be light and the hours as flexible as he pleased. There would be plenty of spare time to develop other dalliances.

The girl also seemed pleased with the arrival of her new companion. She hadn't been all that content with only the old judge and his housekeeper to commune with. He had tended to be a bit dour and impatient with her at times, although he was generally very good to her. The judge, like her own father, was taken up with managing his finances, which seemed to consume most of his time. The housekeeper was very sweet to her, but was kept quite busy with her duties of managing the house.

The girl had told herself that she couldn't complain too bitterly, for it had, after all, become the first real home in her short, dreary fourteen years of life. Now, with the opportunity of new diversions, things seemed to be looking up.

###

The Cartwyth and Dalmkys families had, in better times, been close. It had once been hoped that they could become even closer through a marriage. However, the only elegible Dalmkys woman had found carnal succour with one of her own gender. In any case, Alexander Cartwyth, an only son, had been far too taken up with his lucrative law career to have any time for romantic entanglements, much less marriage.

The only Dalmkys son, Farley, had been married late to a woman of good birth, but almost ten years his senior. Pressure to produce an heir resulted in his wife, Florence, then in her forty-eighth year, giving birth to a daughter, Florina. Though Florence eventually succumbed to complications of the birth and such a late pregnancy, Farley soldiered on, as best he could, with the care and rearing of their daughter. Though he meant well, he had little time for actual parenting. That function was left largely to household staff and Florina's aging grandparents.

Florina had been an angelic and placid child, and a delight to be around. By the time she was about eight, however, Farley was finally forced to acknowledge that she was, as the common folk might put it, four bits shy of a full dollar. Then, after years of financial reverses and his parents' deaths, he no longer had the means or energy to continue caring for her. However, his old friend, Alexander, had agreed to take care of her, after no slight amount of persuasive pleading on Farley's part.

So it was that on her thirteenth birthday, Florina Dalmkys was moved, bag and baggage, to the modest Cartwyth estate on the other side of town. There, she was placed in the care of Gladys Medwyn, the housekeeper. Gladys was a kindly spinster, and though middle aged before her time, she and Florina struck an immediate rapport. The judge, however, wanted it understood that Gladys' duties to him and his home should not suffer because of this girl's presence. As a result, Gladys could not always afford Florina with the attention and companionship of which she was in such need.

With so much time to herself, Florina day-dreamed a lot; and as time wore on, these day-dreams began taking on a sexual tone. Her awakening sexuality became a catalyst for self-exploration, and many a blissful hour was spent thus occupied. Since no one had ever thought to admonish her against forming such habits, and since it felt so good, she reasoned that it was quite natural.

Her first self-induced orgasm had been a little unnerving, but after reflecting on the exquisite sensations, she set out to develop a variety of ways of arriving at and improving on those wondrous feelings.

Her fingers and knuckles, the heel of her foot, and eventually foreign objects were brought into repertoire. One of her favourite items in these dalliances was a bar of soap during her bath times. She found that she could clench it between her upper thighs, and by working her thigh muscles, which would leave her fingers free to fondle her nipples, she could bring herself to orgasm in short order. Occasionally, though, the soap would become so slick that it would pop out of the grasp of her thighs, usually at a crucial moment, and cause her some frustration. A new bar would never give her any problems, though, and the toll on the supply was uncommonly high.

At about this epoch, she happened upon a pair of dogs that were mating at the back of the property. As she couldn't recall ever having witnessed a similar event between animals, or at all for that matter, she found it fascinating. It made her wonder about the human male's function in this regard. She wondered, too, how similar the human male's *apparatus* might be to that of the male dog. Was it every bit as long, and gloriously red? A man was bigger than a dog, so perhaps his *apparatus* would be too. She particularly enjoyed the part where the male dog nuzzled and licked the bitch's parts before he mounted her. What a special thrill that would be to be licked *there*.

That night she dreamed about some faceless boy licking her d*own there*, and awoke in the midst of a shattering orgasm. That was it! She just had to experience that for real. But how, and with whom?

Except for some home schooling that she received by turns from the judge and Gladys, Florina was largely left to her own devices. She read passably well and occasionally foraged through the judge's library for anything suitably interesting. On one of these forays, she came across a couple of books on human anatomy. Not knowing what "anatomy" meant, but impressed by the size of the volumes, she hopefully flipped through the pages. About halfway through the second tome, she came across a whole section full of coloured illustrations, and even some actual photographs, of the human body and its various parts. At long last she had found out what the human male's *apparatus* looked like. Not only that, but also that it could go through various stages from flaccid to tumescent. (She immediately gleaned the meaning of "flaccid" and "tumescent" by the appropriate juxtaposition of the words to the photographs.) What a wondrous thing! It was not, however, gloriously red. It was an enviable instrument, though, that could also apparently vary in length. How absolutely fascinating—and titillating!

Her fourteenth birthday came and went; and although she had enjoyed the little party and lovely presents, she seemed no nearer the fulfillment of her fondest wish.

Then Morlen Quencis arrived.

###

Morlen impatiently awaited his first night alone with a female. During that first day he had walked the grounds with Florina. She had held his hand as they walked and talked of things he didn't recall only seconds later. His mind was on other things, like the feel of her breast when she tucked his hand between her upper arm and body as she held it. For several minutes the feel of that warm, rounded, feminine appendage kindled a warm glow in his loins that he hadn't experienced before. It felt good. At one point, as they sat side by side on a bench at the back of the garden, she had laid his hand, still in her grasp, in her lap. The warmth of her upper thighs, through the thin fabric of her dress, maintained the warm glow in his loins.

Morlen had inched his hand higher, with no noticeable resistance on her part, and felt the gentle roundness of her pubic mound. To the back of his hand, it felt distinctly hot. She seemed not to notice as he, ever so slightly, rubbed the back of his hand across that gentle roundness, and they continued to talk. To a casual eavesdropper, it would have seemed like gibberish they spoke, but to them it didn't matter; it was merely secondary.

As the day began to fade and they walked hand in hand back to the house, Florina had contrived, with sideward swings of her arms, to rub the back of her hand against Morlen's ever increasing tumescence. Morlen's impatience for the night deepened.

When they arrived back at the house, he immediately went to the upstairs bathroom to examine this new phenomenon—his first authentic erection. During his rapt examination, he hadn't noticed that Florina had followed him. Slowly she extended a nervous, quavering hand around to fondle this object of her consuming fascination. At first he was somewhat startled, but as the warm fingers wrapped themselves around his erection, he slowly relaxed and allowed a very pleasant sensation to wash over him.

He turned slowly to face her, and to his astonishment found that she had divested herself of her dress and stood quite naked before him. He reached tentatively for her small breasts, and at the merest touch, her nipples enlarged and grew quite rigid. This, he found to be both intriguing and titillating.

The bedroom intercom sprang to life with Gladys' voice announcing that dinner was being served. Although Morlen's and Florina's hunger now emanated from regions other than their bellies, they hurriedly dressed and descended to the dining room.

Morlen was grateful for his baggy trousers that tended to camouflage his only slightly diminished erection. He was further grateful, after seating himself at the table, that the offending member was then totally hidden from view.

It was a delicious meal, for Gladys was an excellent cook. However, after the dessert had been devoured, neither Morlen nor Florina could have recounted what it had been that they had just eaten. After a seeming eternity of obligatory small talk with the judge and Gladys, Florina arose and helped clear the table. Morlen mumbled something about it having been a tiring day, excused himself to the judge and very untiredly mounted the stairs. The judge, grinning to himself, retired to his study and a glass of creme de menthe.

Upon arriving at their bedroom, Morlen hurriedly doffed his clothes and leapt, completely nude, into the nearest bed. After what seemed an interminable length of time, Florina entered, and in one fluid motion shed her single garment and fairly flew to the bed upon which Morlen lay in fevered anticipation.

In the judge's study, one television monitor, in a bank of six, flickered in full colour with the tableau vivant being played out in an upstairs bedroom. These monitors hadn't been employed for some years, but now the judge congratulated himself on not having had them dismantled and removed. With the study door locked and the monitor sound transferred to an ear piece, the judge would not be interrupted in the enjoyment of this little diversion. He poured himself a large snifter of cognac and settled back in a chaise recliner directly in front of the live monitor.

By the wee hours of the morning, although the antics of the young performers continued only slightly abated, judge Alexander Cartwyth had dozed to a satisfied slumber, with a thin film of perspiration still present on his flushed face.

###

After weeks of the nocturnal cavortings with Florina, it all began to lose it's sparkle, not to say appeal, for Morlen. They had explored each other and each other's cravings until little presented a surprize or much of a thrill anymore. The culminating act was still a great release, but the road to that act no longer offered Morlen any challenge or novelty. He had, he thought, in but a few short weeks, become a man. There wasn't much to it, really; so he decided to move on to other things.

In his spare time, Morlen had also discovered the *cerebral* delights of the judge's library. He had already read volumes on the global financial turmoil. (Things financial had been of acute interest to him for as long as he could remember.) It seemed that the main cause for this turmoil was that individual monetary systems were so disparate that international economic trade was at a veritable standstill. Without this trade, countries could not sustain the value of their own currencies, and the whole thing had become a vicious circle. Individual currencies had long since become cumbersome tools for trade. They had, in effect, become virtually obsolete; and therein lay the crux of the whole problem.

The World Trade Organization, by then a de facto world government, had attempted at length, and in vain, to implement some form of global currency. However, even countries with worthless currencies had jealously clung to them with something that was supposed to pass for nationalism, but was, in fact, a fear of a loss of sovereignty. Morlen viewed this as economic suicide; in short, as lunacy.

The answer, Morlen felt, had to be relatively simple. He had always found that simple solutions had usually proven to work the best. Besides, it seemed to him that the powers that be probably couldn't see the forest for the trees; an assertion that was truer than he realized. So Morlen embarked on a new project—a crusade of sorts.

Credit cards were still widely and, where possible, abundantly used for domestic commerce. Although the average line of credit was a half a million dollars or so, many had long since exceeded that limit in an attempt at maintaining minimum living standards. There was little hope of financial institutions ever collecting much of the estimated three and a quarter trillion dollars of accumulated credit card debt; not only because few could pay, but also because the overloaded and over-hacked computer systems were incapable of rendering intelligible information.

In an effort to ameliorate their difficulties, most United North American financial institutions had continued merging with each other until only two giant corporations remained. However, this succeeded only in increasing the ranks of the unemployed, which, in turn put more pressure on the entire system.

Morlen had pondered the system of credit cards and their uses; but had soon realized that this system would be useless for global commerce. Who, in their right mind, would be willing to advance even more credit in that economic atmosphere. Then, it came to him in a flash: why not set up something like a global credit point system, whereby a certain type and amount of labour or service gleaned the provider a certain number of points. These points could be registered in regional computer banks linked to a central global bank, and used for purchases. Goods worldwide could be point-priced accordingly, and thus the *credit point* would become a unit of global currency.

A certain type of personal identification tool, in existence for over twenty years, came in the form of an *identachip* embedded in the palm of an individual's hand and read by a scanner. These chips were no larger than the head of a tack but could hold tens of thousands of bits of information. Thus far they had been used only by diplomats, heads of state, corporate CEOs and the like. Nothing, however, could prevent them from being generally used, and they would be more secure than cards that could be lost or stolen.

It would be a relatively simple matter to incorporate credit point information into these *identachips*. Upon verification by scanner, an individual, or a corporate purchaser could purchase anything he or his corporation could afford, anywhere in the world.

Morlen's mind fairly hummed with the import of these ideas. He must draw up a plan or proposal and present it to someone who had political connections. Judge Alexander Cartwyth would do for a start. Who else would listen to a twelve year old farmer's son?

The whole idea felt like magic—and it worked like magic on Morlen's libido. That night his carnal cravings reached new heights, much to the delight of Florina—and the judge.

The World Infotel News Network flashed the news that at long last the beginning of monetary stability was at hand. It was reported that a retired judge, one Alexander Cartwyth, and a young protege had developed a revolutionary global monetary system based on a credit point device; and that the pressure on the WTO to accept and implement this idea was mounting. It further reported that the credit point device required the implantation of personal identification chips, and the development of a global, as well as regional, data banks to record and correlate earnings and expenditures. Eventually, it was indicated, it would be crucial that everyone have an embedded identification chip from birth to death. It did, in fact, become mandatory.

The undertaking was monumental, so it had been decided that the Global Defence League was the only organization that had the wherewithal to implement it.

The GDL had come into being in 2024 with the melding of the crumbling United Nations, the North Atlantic Treaty Organization and organizations of that ilk. It was closely linked to the World Trade Organization, and had massive and wide ranging resources.

The WTO had set itself the task of regulating income and pricing guidelines; while the GDL undertook the task of creating a network force of medical and paramedical personnel for the purpose of identachip implantations. Many of the long-disused government facilities were then equipped to accommodate these operations.

Biotech Corporation International, a large conglomerate of a hundred and twelve biotechnical companies, was contracted to produce ten billion of the identachips, with a further three billion to be produced as needed. Their mandate also included the development, production and distribution of appropriate scanning devices.

International legislation had been drafted, passed and implemented to the effect that within two years each and every person must be implanted and registered with a regional data bureau. These data bureaus had the task of imprinting all the required information onto the imbedded chips, and activating the individual accounts for their district of authority. Thereafter, the data, thus processed, was also to be filed with the Global Data Authority in the European capitol at Brussels. The wheels were in full motion. Never before had bureaucracies been seen to accomplish so much in such a short space of time.

By November of 2040 every one of the world's six billion, three hundred and eighty-four million, six hundred and thirty-six thousand, seven hundred and ninety-seven men, women and children above the age of one year, had been implanted and processed.

Judge Alexander Cartwyth was ecstatic; especially when he received the e-mail transmission informing him that he and young Morlen had been chosen as co-recipients of the Nobel Prize for Humanitarian Accomplishments, concurrent with a two million point credit deposited into their new accounts.

For Morlen's part, he was somewhat overwhelmed by the whole flow of events of the previous two years. Intellect aside, he was, after all, a fourteen year old farmer's son, and quite impressed by the whirlwind into which he had been caught up. However, he was eagerly anticipating the trip abroad and investment of the Nobel Prize (the share in two million point credits wasn't disappointing either).

Morlen's only regret in all of this was that the judge had steadfastly refused to allow Florina along. Over the preceding year, Morlen had grown quite fond of her. Aside from her voracious appetite for sex, Morlen had found that she had an inquiring and active mind that appealed to him. In spite of himself, Morlen, in fact, was falling in love.

Under Gladys' tutelage, Florina had become a good cook, an adept baker and an able aide to Gladys in keeping the house in good order. These attributes, however, weren't deemed, by the judge, to be sufficient prerequisites for the trip. Also, he secretly felt that she may

embarrass him with her seeming simple mindedness. So at home she
would stay.

In the end, Morlen was left only with trying to assuage Florina's
disappointment by indulging her more in her favourite passtimes, and
impressing on her that their absence would be for only a week or so.

By the time that Morlen and the judge had boarded the old Boeing
818, Florina had been mollified sufficiently to shed only a few tears at
their departure. Then it was back home to her bar of soap at bath
times, and other devices "for a week or so".

Gladys swore to herself that Florina must be the cleanest young
woman in the whole state of Manitoba.

The Beginning—

DICK AND JANE

After suffering through years of insanely jealous outbursts from his wife, Dick Bradigan had finally been forced into having her committed indefinitely to a psychiatric hospital. As stressful as bearing the wildly irrational accusations had been for him, he could have and would have coped had it not been for their young daughter. Six year old Felicity deserved a safer and more stable childhood.

Dick had always thought that he and Jane had an idyllic marriage; and they did, in the beginning at least. At the outset, Jane had been a loving and passionate wife, and their first year of marriage was nothing if not blissful.

Although their wedding had been a small, quiet affair, with only their two remaining family members and a few close friends, the honeymoon had been a spectacular event. The lovingly erotic abandonment with which it proceeded was something that neither had ever experienced, and they had vowed it would never end.

The setting, on Rarotonga in the Cook Islands, was certainly condusive to romance, but it had been more than merely that. There had been a deep mutual love commingled with an almost unquenchable physical lust from the very beginning of their relationship.

When they had returned after two weeks in the sunny climes of the South Pacific, their friends had teased them about their lack of tans. But Mr. and Mrs. Richard Bradigan had just snuggled close and laughed with them. Their love for each other was an open book and they didn't care who read the pages.

It was of little surprize to anyone who read those pages, that about three months after their nuptials, Jane announced that there would soon be a new twig on the Bradigan family tree. Everyone was ecstatic for them, and Jane fairly glowed in anticipation.

Before Jane had announced the news generally, she had hardly been able to contain her excitement until Dick came home. Wouldn't you just know it, she had thought to herself, it had to be one of Dick's late nights, too. When he had finally arrived and heard Jane's breathlessly delivered news, Dick had been giddy with love and wonder and a hundred other feelings that flooded through him. This gorgeous creature was going to make him a father, and he loved her more than he could ever express in mere words. So, with tears of unbounded joy coursing down his cheeks, he had kissed her and poured his heart and soul into it until he thought he would implode.

"My god but I love you, Dickie!" Jane had said. "Do you think it's too late to add a feature or two to our little package?"—And they had made love, there and then, on the diningroom table.

Then, shortly after Felicity was born, it had all begun to crumble, and the unfounded jealousy and accusations began, and escalated. The escalation was slow at first, but seemed to gain momentum as time wore on.

He still loved Jane dearly, but her last outburst had bordered on homicidal. Dick became afraid of what she might do while he was at work. He had already begun noticing signs of unusual petulance directed at Felicity. This angelic child, the spit of her mother, was supposed to have been such an unparalleled joy to them both, but now he was beginning to have some serious doubts about Jane's feelings.

"You fornicating bastard! You just want me out of the way so you can bring your sluts home with you. I'd kill my girl and cut you where it hurts the most before I'd let that happen."

That had been the last thing that Jane said to him before they strapped her to the gurney and trundled her away. It tended only to confirm his fears about Jane's growing animosity towards Felicity, and justify the most difficult decision he'd ever had to make.

After a spell of treatments, Dick was allowed to visit Jane for an hour once a week. Those visits, however, always turned out either sullen and silent or wildly acrimonious affairs, regardless of Dick's attempts at pleasantries. She had even accused him of incest with his sister, Helen.

"Perhaps you could plonk a baby into Helen. Lord knows that china-balled husband of hers hasn't been able to," she had said.

He loved Jane so much. How could she talk to him that way? All her treatments and medications didn't seem to be doing much good. Dick remembered that the doctors had said it may take awhile, but still . . .

"Why don't you just bugger off home and boink someone now that you've got all this free time to youself," she'd usually say towards the end of a visit.

# # #

Dick's younger sister, Helen, and her husband, Mark, had been together for five years, and had pined every minute of that period at not being able to become parents. Mark's frequent absences with the military had certainly been part of the problem, but apparently not the entire problem.

Since infertility seemed to have been a possibility, Mark had told Helen that he had been examined by a military medical specialist and declared to be completely capable of becoming a father. Helen, for her own secret reasons, had her doubts. Although those doubts were entirely unfounded, she preferred them to what the alternative would have to be. She had resented the implication.

Helen, in her early thirties, wanted desperately to be a mother, and was painfully aware of her biological clock ticking away its advantage. In the meantime she took every opportunity of playing surrogate mother to her niece, Felicity. The warm, maternal glow that she always felt when Felicity stayed over had an almost narcotic effect. Therefore, she had always made a special effort to stay on good terms with Jane so that the source of those feelings would not be denied to her.

Helen had even tried visiting Jane in the hospital, but with explosive results.

"Don't think I don't know what you and Dick the prick get up to while Mark's away so much. Scratches your itch pretty good, does he?" Jane had shrieked.

"Please, Jane! That's just not true. Dick loves you so very much. And think about your little girl," Helen had tearfully replied.

At that, Jane got strangely quiet and said, "Just piss off, you scheming slut. You might have my husband warming your bed, but you're not going to get my little girl too."

Even aside from the grip of her most manic episodes, Jane felt an inexplicable distrust of her sister-in-law's motives. It was intuitive more than anything she could put her finger on; but it persisted nevertheless.

# # #

From time to time, it was necessary for Dick to work late. When those occasions arose, Helen would pick Felicity up from school, feed her, play with her and keep her overnight. It was a good arrangement. Helen loved the company, with her own husband away in the military, and Dick didn't have to scramble at the last minute to find a sitter. Helen's and Mark's place was only three blocks away and closer to the school, so that was convenient as well.

On one such night, after a particularly long day, Dick arrived home dog tired. As he entered the darkened house, his senses inexplicably began tingling, and the fine hairs on his arms and back of his neck stood erect. He felt something was amiss; but what? The door had been securely locked. Could someone have found that spare key under the loose flagstone at the front door?

"Nah!" he said to himself. "Who would ever think to look there. Besides, a burglar would just break a window or kick in a door."

He shook his head to try and dispel an almost eerie feeling.

"Just a cool draft," he thought; "and I am beat."

But he couldn't so easily quell the sense that something wasn't quite right, so he checked the back door. It was secure, as were the ground floor windows. He thought that maybe all he really needed was a stiff drink and a good night's sleep. He had grabbed a bite on the way home, so at least he wouldn't have to fix anything now but that drink. He made a mental note to check the upstair windows before he went to bed.

With his Scotch/rocks in his hand, he switched on the T.V. to catch the news final at eleven and unwind a bit.

As the anchorman's voice announced the escape of a potentially violent patient from St. Alexandra's Psychiatric Hospital, something again niggled at Dick's senses.

Then, it was just *one* sense. The unmistakable scent of Anais Anais was present; *her* favourite scent.

Then another sense came into play. A faint sound, as of a slippered foot brushing a carpeted stair. Then a slight creak of a stair; the third stair from the bottom, Dick knew.

Dick wheeled around in the chair just in time to glimpse a figure hurtling towards him, hair flying wildly, crazily on her head. A long nightgown pressed seductively to the curves of her body; that body that he knew so well. Something in an upraised hand glinted light reflected from the T.V. screen.

"No, Ja—!"

A shriek broke what remained of the stillness. A splintering crash and a sharp, searing flash followed. Then deep, engulfing silence and darkness ensued.

# # #

"What a helluva mess," said a corporal from the local R.C.M.P. detachment. "This poor bastard's got an eight inch butcher knife jammed in his chest, and the nutty cow that did it must've tripped or been shoved; slammed her head clean through the television and fried herself. What a freakin', bloody mess!"

"Alright, corporal;" said the coroner, "we can all see the picture."

The coroner's perpetually sad eyes surveyed the scene. Most of the death scenes he had attended in his thirty-seven years as district coroner had been disquieting, but this one was particularly so.

He had known Dick and Jane since they were school kids. He had watched them grow up, fall in love, marry and start a family. Hadn't he been the one to give Jane away at their wedding—a stand-in for a long dead father? Now this.

There was such a myriad of complications that could visit each marriage; but when marriage started with such a strong and obvious mutual love and devotion, you would think that it would have, at the very least, a fighting chance.

"Fate is a bastard," he thought aloud.

"Whatzat?" inquired the corporal, just on his way out.

"Hmm? Oh nothing; nothing at all." replied the coroner.

After a constable had imparted the sad news to Helen, asked a few perfunctory questions and left, she couldn't help a satisfied little giggle to herself. It had all turned out so much better than she could ever have hoped. Now, they were *both* dead, and there wasn't any blood on *her* hands after all. The little girl would be her's; her's and Mark's. Mark could no longer condemn her, albeit silently, for not being able to have a child of her own.

Time, that avaricious thief of all things, had not been on her side; had been against her from the start. She knew that she would have been capable of murder, even fratricide, if need be, to satisfy that burning need that had been with her for so long. That need that consumed most of her waking hours.

This child, while not of her body, was at least of her blood. She had adored and coveted Felicity from the first glimpse of her in the maternity ward.

Jane, that abrasive bitch, didn't deserve to be a mother, Helen felt. The proof of that had been witnessed over the past six years. And that spineless, simpering brother of hers had allowed it to drag on for all that time; all that precious time that could have been for her and Felicity.

How she had loathed their good fortune, and her bad. How she had loathed having to toady to them for their vapid magnanimity. How she had loathed having to bring Felicity back to her *parent's* house after an all too short visit. But, at last, at long last, that was all behind her now. No more toadying; no more returning to a childless home; no more empty dreams and unfulfilled yearnings. She would be a mother at last; at long, long last.

She *could* be a mother too; a *good* mother. She would show them. She would show them all. Yes she would!

The End?

THE KEY TO CONTENTMENT

I, Claibourne T. Hollincrutz, being of sound mind (*I am so!*) do herewith submit the following for the edification of the reader, and to glean the validation of genius that is only *my* rightful due.

When I had finished the original draft of this piece, it was in excess of 1200 pages. It dealt to a large degree with the philosophy of contentment. Well, as anyone who has ever studied philosophy can attest, there are no definitive answers, only questions. But I *knew* that I had the definitive answer. Therefore, a rewrite was imperative.

Also, after proof reading the work, I realized that it may not be what the seeker of contentment would thank me for offering. Seekers of contentment tend to be in rather a hurry, and become testy and sometimes downright surly when faced with such an impediment to speedy gratification.

With this in mind, I rewrote the whole damned tome with a view to condensing it a bit while maintaining all of the salient points. The result is, as you will see, an undeniably manageable work that cuts right through the usual ultra professional and philosophical baffle-gab and hits right to the heart and soul of the subject.

The first two chapters deal with how contentment is generally perceived by each gender in turn. The third chapter undoubtedly succeeds in conciliating these two seemingly disparate perceptions into one cohesive entity that both genders will find contentment with.

Read on then, and marvel at the insight, and unbounded genius!

Men, some to bus'ness, some to Pleasure take;
But every Woman is at heart a Rake;
Men, some to Quiet, some to public Strife;
But ev'ry Lady would be Queen for life.

—Alexander Pope
1688-1744.

CHAPTER ONE

Men's Contentment

* Cook for us.

* Make enthusiastic love to us.

* Beyond that, just allow us the unfettered opportunity to be ourselves.

CHAPTER TWO

Women's Contentment

* Obey us like a mother.
* Baby and protect us like a daughter.
* Give us economic security like a wife (giving us at least 50% of the credit for the results of your labors).
* Trouble us just enough to have an excuse to nag (keeping life interesting for us), but not enough to really piss us off. Keep the balance or lose the game!
* Give us the opportunity (we'll take it anyway) to fulfill ourselves with a job/career (read: a paid social-interaction hobby, where we either hate with a passion or love and admire and empathize with our co-workers—there can be no grey areas for us).
* Having done that, you had better take over (and appear genuinely glad of the chance) at least 50% of the household chores, which, of course, try as you may, you'll never meet our standards at. All this notwithstanding the fact that you work 40 to 50 hours per week (earning 80% of the total family income) and do all of the external house and yard maintenance.
* Love our dear friends (read: acquaintances and co-workers—those that we love and admire and empathize with) and gleefully visit and interact with them even though the very thought of them constricts your bowels with nausea. You, of course, may have no personal friends of which we don't wholeheartedly approve (good luck!).
* Should all the foregoing (and more, as we see fit from time to time) meet with our complete approval (again, good luck!), then, and only then, will we allow you uncomplaining access to our

bodies. We may even enjoy that, although you'll never know for sure. Our sexual enjoyment, in long terms, is only distantly secondary to our prime agenda, namely biological completion; i.e.: motherhood within a secure environment of our own engineering (and your labor). Any enjoyment is only an added bonus.

CHAPTER THREE

The Key

Simply put, mixed gender societies just don't work. They need complete restructuring.

It is, I believe, blatantly obvious from the vast differences between the gender-specific perceived contentments mentioned in previous chapters, that it would be virtually and realistically impossible to expect men and women to continue to cohabit and simultaneously be content. Therefore, in my considered opinion, it is of the utmost importance and, indeed, mandatory to continued survival of civilized society, that living arrangements be altered as follows: that women live on one side of a street and men on the opposite facing side of the street, whether in single family dwellings or apartment complexes.

When a *service* is required by a man of a woman, or vice-versa, he or she merely crosses the street within their block and knocks at the appropriate door. Going to other streets or other blocks would only be tolerated by law when the required service could not be performed by someone in your own street or block. Otherwise such an infraction would be viewed by law and society at large in much the same way as adultery is currently viewed, and an appropriate law suit would, of necessity, ensue.

Such cross-street visitations would be limited to one, two hour period per day, and would be verifiable by punch cards issued on a calendar-monthly basis. Upon a visitor's acceptance, punch cards would be exchanged, punched and then returned upon termination of the visit. Any more punch holes in a punch card than there were days in that particular month would be grimly viewed. Such an infraction would be dealt with by withholding the following month's punch card. Surprize checks by punch card inspectors would keep everyone on their toes, and would virtually insure honesty.

Overnight visitations would be permitted between two individuals of opposite gender and who were in agreement, as long as the total duration of the visit did not exceed twelve consecutive hours between 7:00 p.m. and 7:00 a.m. on the following day, and that the appropriate punch holes appeared on both individuals' punch cards. Such overnight visitations must not exceed one per calendar month. The very fabric of society would depend on it. Should such overnight visitations occur in three consecutive calendar months between two unmarried members of the opposite gender, a state of common-law marriage would be deemed to have occurred and the appropriate legalities would be implied.

Individuals would maintain the right to wed a like-minded person of the opposite gender, but constant cohabitation would be expressly forbidden. Such an antisocial act would have to be carried on outside of the city's limits. Again, the very fabric of civilized society would depend on it.

The children of married (or common-law) couples could freely visit and/or stay with either parent until the age of 18 years, at which time punch cards would be issued to them and the visitations rules of decent society would apply.

The only exception to the visitation and cohabitation rules would be extended to bonafide tourists (whether foreign or domestic), who, should they insist on such barbarism as constant cohabitation, would be allowed to indulge themselves in their deviant behaviour. The resultant stress and turmoil between such cohabiting tourist couples would serve as a keen lesson to those more civilized inhabitants of the neighborhood.

There then, in a nutshell, is the key not only to contentment, but perhaps even bliss and ultimately world peace.

The End

PONDERINGS IN PARANOIA AND OTHER FOOD FOR THOUGHT

Number One.

The internal convolutions and illogic of the bureaucratic mind, being what it is, has left me startled and deeply disturbed to discover how extremely difficult it would be for me to prove conclusively that I, in fact, am me should my birth and social insurance records be irretrievably lost.

By a laboriously circuitous process of elimination, I would first have to show that I was no one else who had ever lived in my lifetime (or estimated lifetime, because my actual age would also be in serious question). In the process of accomplishing that end, however, many would have died and many others would have been born. Therefore, it would also be necessary to show that I was not any of them either.

Having finally arrived at the end of this Hurculean labour and proved (at least to myself) that I am not anyone else who ever lived in my (estimated) lifetime, I would be left with just this: I am most likely not anyone else, therefore the preponderance of evidence (allowing for a virtually inevitable margin of error) would suggest that I, in fact, am me—perhaps.

There could, of course, be no definitive conclusions drawn, because bureaucrats, being what and how they are, would question my *unofficial* evidence ad nauseum et infinitum—or simply reject it all out-of-hand, as is frequently their wont.

On the up side of all of this, I would never have to pay taxes again—HMMM! Now there's food for thought . . .

Number Two:

Sitting alone here in my cell, I have had ample time to think about and wonder at all the abstractions that life has to offer. My own life was something of an abstraction—my life on the outside, that is. In here it is all calm and serene, for abstractions (even mild ones) tend to excite the inmates to mayhem (and worse).

I was, in the outside world, an outwardly respected and popular member of our close-knit little community. All my life, whatever I said or did evoked the utmost interest and attention of the community. My every word and deed was regarded as some precious gem, although I was not of an important office or station.

Ours was a community of thoughtful, caring folk; folk who practised tolerance to perhaps an extreme. Of course, I was not particularly aware of this at the time. When you are born into a situation and never experience anything else, you believe that the whole world is as what you know. That was the case with me until the Grunderschloffs came to our town. She was to be our new school teacher and he was a clinical psychologist on sabatical to write a treatise or some such dissertation on his own greatness in the field.

It was on the eve of my twenty-eighth birthday that the tolerance sodden bottom fell out of my comfortable little world. It wasn't until much later, after I had been safely tucked away into a new little world, that I found out the truth. Doctor/Professor Maximillian von Helsing-Grunderschloff had determined that I had the mental age of a five year old; thereby placing me beneath the developemental level of an imbecile. Also, due to my size and prodigious physical strength, I was deemed to be a danger to society.

I have to wonder: why am I in an asylum? Am I insane? I don't feel insane. How does insanity feel? Boy, these funny long sleeved jackets that buckle in the back sure are warm—and itchy.

My father is writing this for me, because he never acquired a taste for eating pencils or drinking ink.

How well our closest family and friends look after us!

Are your family and friends looking after you?

Number Three.

At the time of writing this, there exists, at the Bell Telephone System Laboratory in Murray Hill, New Jersey, a room referred to as a "dead room". It is not a room for "dead" files or "dead" bits of telephone equipment—or even the dead bodies of those recalcitrants who had neglected paying their service bills. It is a room for or of "dead" sound.

At the time of writing, this "dead room" was reputedly the most anechoic room in the world, eliminating some 99.98 percent of reflected sound. Now, since what we normally hear is a result of r*eflected* sound, we could conceivably stand in the middle of this room shouting our lungs out and, presumeably, hear nary a whisper.

Knowing full well that your hearing is perfect, consider for a moment the sensation of not being able to hear a sound—any sound; a sound that you know perfectly well should be there, because you've just initiated the physical catalyst that would normally have resulted in sound waves entering your perfectly functioning inner ears, resulting in the realization of sound. Yet there is no sound. There should be sound, but there isn't.

Now consider having to cope with this situation for days, weeks, months or even years.

Total sensory deprivation can do strange things to the human mind in only a matter of minutes. But of all the senses, hearing can have the greatest impact, either by its acuity or its sudden absence. A person in solitary confinement can exist relatively comfortably for some length of time with but the sound of his own voice; but consider that same solitude with absolutely no sound.

One has one's thoughts of course, but it's hardly the same. Besides, after a time those thoughts tend to lose lucidity unless augmented by outside stimuli.

What an absolutely Machiavellian way to *encourage* information out of an individual; or *encourage* a particular ideological adherence into one.

I wonder if the CIA knows about this—or al Kaida . . .

Number Four:

This really has nothing whatever to do with paranoia; so I guess it must fall under the subtitle of: "and other food for thought". It was really quite clever of me to think of making *and other food for thought* part of the title, wasn't it? It's almost as though I knew what I was doing, don't you think? But I digress.

This is about the old philosophical question: *If a tree falls in the forest and no one is present to hear it, does it make a sound?* There doesn't ever seem to have been any recorded answer(s) to such a, dare I say, profound question. There should surely have been some answer generated by such a philosophical exercise over such a period of time. The question does give the impression of being ageless. To my mind it also gives the impression of being generated by someone who had far too much time on his hands and far too little else to think about. However, I do digress, yet again.

Here, then, you lucky devils, is the definitive answer:

All things, tangible or not, are deemed to exist because they are *perceived* to exist. Perception has a variety of components, namely the five senses and that greater part of knowledge referred to as memory. At least one of these components must be triggered for the object, tangible or not, to be perceived to exist, and therefore to *actually* exist for all intents and purposes. Hence, nothing can be deemed to exist without the ability to be perceived.

Now, just because all of the elements (save one) in our tree-falling-in-the-forest scenario are present to create a sound, doesn't mean that a sound can be deemed to exist. The one element that is *not* present, namely the element of perception (i.e.: the ear and all of its internal receptor components), is the only one that could render the hypothesis into fact. Therefore, the only answer to this age old question has got to be an unequivocal and resounding *no*.

I've now and forever put an end to that bit of nonsense.

Now, aren't you glad you read these pages?

Number Five:

I have a theory on time dimensions, which is ultimately, though also not necessarily, connected to time travel. For those readers who may be interested, I would like to share this theory with you. The rest of you may take a television break.

At the outset I should say that what I *don't* know about quantum physics would fill a sizeable tome indeed. What does intrigue me, though, and something I think I know a little about, is the possibility of time travel and what I think is an intrinsic component—namely alternate time dimensions.

As I understand Einstein's theory, the closer we get to the speed of light the slower actual time passes (time being an elastic component of the space-time continuum). At the actual speed of light, time literally stands still. Beyond the speed of light, time starts a reverse course—namely starts going backwards.

(Pretty heady stuff, isn't it?)

It has been suggested that eventually time travel will be possible—in *both* directions. That is to say backwards as well as forwards. Now, to go *back* in time, as already mentioned, one must exceed the speed of light, which would seem to indicate that to go *forward* in time one would have to reverse the procedure to the point where one was going slower than stop—hmmm! That's a pretty tough concept to grasp, and would seem to be possible only after death.

Suppose for the moment that we are in that distant future where time travel exists (the mind can be a wonderful time machine) and we take a trip back five hours or five years—it matters little because for us that time would no longer exist. To highlight that point, let me put it this way: you go back to whenever within your own lifetime and meet up with yourself. (This is getting headier all the time.) You would very likely not be able to interact with yourself because had you experienced that interaction, it would most assuredly have created a memory that you would most certainly recall by virtue of it being such an unusual occurance. Therefore, it is highly unlikely that any interaction with the past would be possible—very fortunately, I think. Just imagine the possible and perhaps cataclysmic ramifications of interactions with the past.

As to alternate dimensions, it has been suggested (and very occasionally outrightly stated) that there are a finite number of dimensions, i.e. 4 or 5 or 12, etc. Well, at the risk of sounding captious, I feel that these suggestions and statements are fallacious nonsense put forward by sophists who lack the imagination and the power of reason, and the tenacity required to amalgamate the two in proportions necessary for cohesive scientific theory.

This is where my theory concerning alternate dimensions comes in. It goes something like this: it's my contention that there are as many dimensions as there have been moments in time. We, at the present moment, are at the head of the time continuum—the future simply does not exist.

Each moment in time represents a dimension entirely separate from the one before. Occasionally, due to some weak area in the space-time continuum (fabric, if you will), a previous dimension may *bleed* through to the present. This may well account for such manifestations as "ghosts" or other hitherto unexplained "visions".

An obvious question that I can almost hear the reader asking is: "How long is a moment?" Well, due to the theoretical elasticity of time, it could virtually be any length. You must remember that our general concept of time is largely governed by chronometers that break time into very convenient as well as strict segments (seconds, minutes, hours), and by calendars that break time into equally convenient and strict segments (days, weeks, months, years). There are no known time measuring instruments that can define a moment or instant. Although these two epithets leave us with a connotation of a very fleeting interval of time, it is by no means certain that they are either fleeting or equal in constancy—given the theoretical elasticity of time.

I could go on at some length to explore another notion that time may not be correctly defined as having only length, but may itself be multi-dimensional. However, food for thought that it may be, my immediate concern was to put forward a single theory. That this theory may well be an integral segment of something larger will undoubtedly be fodder for future think tanks of quantum physics theorists.

Number Six:

To my conscious knowledge, no one wants to kill me. I have led such an innocuous, almost insignificant, life that I cannot for the life of me believe that anyone would wish to deprive me of it. Yet, one night, while in a deep sleep upon my tick pallet, a voice came to me. Oh no, not a deep, sepulchral voice; just a very ordinary, almost kindly voice. It spoke thusly to me in an ancient style of speech:

"To them that would forsooth deprive me of my simple life, I would thus say: if thou art strongly determined enough to have it, then thou wilt surely take it; but also take heed—for it is but a small thing, and small things are easily lost."

I awoke immediately and wrote it down, word for word, as I had heard it, and while it was still fresh in my mind.

Do dreams have specific meanings? Is my life so "small" that it could be "easily lost"? I must endeavour to do more with my life—I must! I must give my life meaning and scope and volume, and such significance that it will not be so easily lost. This will I do, then— beginning today. The world shall know the name of Grigori Yefimovich Novikh—*Rasputin.*

March, 1890.

Number Seven:

Since time immemorial the definition—a definite, unequivocal definition—of *love* has eluded Mankind.

Most dictionaries have this to say about love: as a noun it means: "affection; strong liking; good will; benevolence; charity; devoted attachment to one of the opposite sex; the object of affection;" etc., etc. As a transitive verb it means: "to show affection for; to be delighted with; to admire passionately;" etc., etc., As an intransitive verb it means: "to be in love or to delight." In short, dictionaries say a lot but really don't seem to answer the question—at least with regard to the emotion that binds two people into a sexual relationship.

We may legitimately say of dear, close friends, of either gender, that we love them; meaning that we "show affection for them", "are delighted with them", or "admire them passionately". This, however, does not necessarily mean that we would want to have sexual relations with them. In other words we may be passionate about them, or more accurately about their attributes or abilities, without having the slightest desire for carnal knowledge of them.

Then what is it that determines that we would wish to have carnal knowledge of (make *love* to) that person that we love? Frankly, it's the same thing that determines that we would wish to have carnal knowledge of anyone regardless of feelings of love. It's because of another four lettered word beginning with "L". That word, of course, is *lust.*

Unfortunately that word has acquired something of a bad reputation for no justifiable reason. Let's look at what most dictionaries have to say about *lust.* As a noun it means: "a longing desire; a sexual appetite; craving". As an intransitive verb it means: "to desire passionately; to have sexual appetites". That kind of reminds one of that other four lettered "L" word, doesn't it?

The adverb *passionately* is used in the definitions of both love and *lust.* Let's see what most dictionaries have to say, then, about *passion.* As a noun it means: "intense emotion as of—love; eager desire". There can be no question, then, that there is a clear connection between at least some type of *love* and *lust.* That type of love must surely be the one that exists between two lovers, whether or not they be husband and wife.

I think, therefore, that we can begin to understand that lust, excited into existence by pheromones for example, must be the catalyst for what later becomes the romantic notion of love.

The fact that *lust* has long been almost a dirty word has kept romantics from admitting that their idea of *romantic* love is actually the desire for *carnal* love generated by lust.

Let's face it, it's hardly a revelation that the urge for sexual gratification is the most naturally powerful urge in the animal kingdom. It's right up there with the urge for survival, which is hardly surprizing, as these urges are inextricably linked. Animals (including

Mankind) have killed for sexual gratification, which historically was the only way of passing on genetic material and of survival of the species.

Although Mankind is not the only animal that mates for life (at least theoretically), it is the one to whom *love* has been attributed as being the reason behind it. This seems a rather hubristic view, as true emotions are not subject to conscious generation. I don't believe that it can be argued, with any serious conviction, that romantic (sexual) love isn't generated by lust to at least some degree.

True love, that is the kind of love that binds two people over a long period, has as much to do with respect and trust as it has with lust for sexual union. However, respect and trust take a lot longer to develop than does sexual attraction. Were that not the case, most people would find it impossible to *fall in love* more than once; and as most of us have seen, either personally or through various media, falling in love more than once happens with a rather high degree of frequency.

In the final analysis then, lust, i.e.: sexual attraction, is the genesis of *romantic* love, while respect, trust, etc. is the sustenance by which it survives. There can be no one or two word definition for this type of love that is clearly too complex for that narrow a view.

Now I *know* you're glad that you read on!

Number Eight.

Finally, I think I will leave you with an ancient riddle. Well, actually I don't *think* I will leave you with it; I *know* I will leave you with it, because I am the author, after all. (Some may call me a pedant just because I want to be precise. Well a fig for them!)

The solution to this riddle may hold the key to unlock all the mysteries of the universe; or the solution may simply be the key to a profound personal sense of satisfaction. It may mean nothing or it may mean everything. That will be for you to discover once you have solved the riddle.

Here, then, is the riddle called Riddle-Me-Ree:

> I sit on a rock whilst I'm raising the wind,
> But the storm once abated, I'm gentle and kind.
> I've kings at my feet who await but my nod,
> To kneel in the dust on the ground I have trod.
> Though seen to the world, I'm known to but few;
> The Gentiles detest me, I'm pork to the Jew.
> I've never passed but one night in the dark,
> And that was with Noah alone in the Ark.
> My weight is three pounds, my length is a mile,
> And when I'm discovered you'll say with a smile,
> That my first and my last are the best in our Isle.

No, I cannot present you with the solution—I'm not even certain that it would be allowed. The solution must be the result of your own efforts. I do know, however, that I may give you one clue: the Isle referred to in the last line of Riddle-Me-Ree is British. Now the rest should be easy. Have fun and good luck!

The Very End

—*Really!*